CHRISTMAS IN WILLOW HEIGHTS

WILLOW HEIGHTS SERIES BOOK THREE

ABIGAIL BECK

CHAPTER 1

ary Elle stood at the stove, stirring her special hot chocolate mixture with a secret ingredient, mascarpone. She added mascarpone to her hot chocolate mixture, making her hot chocolate velvety and decadent. Mary Elle had read in a magazine that all the fancy restaurants always added mascarpone to their hot chocolate, so she started adding it to hers. She felt that the mascarpone elevated the taste.

She kept stirring while waiting for Rita to finish her call with her realtor, Mrs. Klein. After announcing Bob's retirement during Thanksgiving dinner, the Holloways found their new home in Willow Heights.

"Hi, Mrs. Klein; thanks for returning my call. I was calling to thank you for helping us find our new home. We're also excited about selling our current home. We packed most of our belongings and can't wait for the open house this weekend."

"It's my pleasure, Mrs. Holloway."

"Oh, please call me Rita."

"Rita, it's my pleasure, and I can't wait to help you with the staging for this weekend."

"We look forward to seeing you once again; thank you," Rita said as she ended the call.

Rita and Bob wanted to retire and move into a smaller house as they were empty nesters. Rita longed to spend more time with Bob, who had worked as a traveling sales associate and business consultant for all of their marriage.

Their new house in Willow Heights was a modest home with three bedrooms and two bathrooms. It also had a big backyard and was near Main Square. The cherry on top was that it was just down the block from Mary Elle's house and three blocks away from Melanie's home. Melanie was Mary Elle's middle child. She moved to Willow Heights a few months ago after separating from her husband.

While house shopping, Rita's only request was to have a big backyard for all her plants and Penny, their chunky little corgi, to get her daily exercise. Bob's only request had been to have a room he could convert into his man cave.

Mrs. Klein had quickly found a few houses, and while they had liked them all, they chose the place closest to Mary Elle and Melanie. The newly engaged Mary Elle was ecstatic to have Rita, her best friend, move to Willow Heights. Since a young age, they had both dreamed of being neighbors, and now it was a reality.

Soon, they would be able to walk to each other's homes. They couldn't wait to make plans for the upcoming Holidays, which were their favorites out of all the holidays. They were eager to decorate and start planning their annual Christmas party with Christmas on its way.

"Here you go, neighbor," Mary Elle said as she placed a Christmas mug full of hot chocolate in front of Rita.

Mary Elle used any excuse to decorate for all holidays, but Christmas was her favorite. She got all her Christmas décor out as soon as Thanksgiving was over. Maybe she didn't even wait for Thanksgiving to pass, but she couldn't help herself. This is Christmas we're talking about.

"Thanks, neighbor," Rita said as she placed her hands around the mug for warmth. "It's only a few degrees colder here than Atlanta, but it feels cooler, doesn't it?"

"Yes, I think it's because we're at a higher altitude here. Let me add some more wood to the furnace. I'll be right back."

On her way to the basement, Mary Elle ran into her sister DeeAnn. She had just woken up and tied her curly hair in a big bun. Unlike Mary Elle, who was always up before the crack of dawn, DeeAnn enjoyed her sleep, and on the weekends, they rarely saw her around until after 11 AM.

"Good morning, sleepyhead! If you'd like a cup, there's some hot chocolate in the kitchen." Mary Elle said.

"Thanks, you know I can't resist your special hot chocolate," DeeAnn said as she walked to the kitchen.

Mary Elle overheard Rita telling DeeAnn about finding a house in Willow Heights. DeeAnn congratulated her, and they made plans to go on a daily evening walk for exercise now that they lived on the same street.

Growing up, the three had been very close. DeeAnn was younger than Rita and Mary Elle, and they had both dotted on her to no end when they were younger. However, everything changed one day when DeeAnn pushed them away. Neither of them knew why and although they tried their best to understand what had gone wrong, their young minds could never wrap their heads around it.

It wasn't until a little over a year ago that DeeAnn came clean to Mary Elle. She told her she'd pushed her away because she found out their mother had an affair, and she was a product of that.

DeeAnn had feared Mary Elle would push her away,

which resulted in DeeAnn pushing her away first. Even though it'd been months since it had all come to light, Mary Elle still had a hard time wrapping her mind around it.

After DeeAnn told her everything, they'd never really talked about it again. She was sure that DeeAnn still had some unresolved issues to deal with, but she would let her open up in her own time.

When Mary Elle returned to the kitchen, she found DeeAnn and Rita on the back deck.

"What are you two up to?" She said as she closed the French doors behind her.

"Rita was just going over what she plans to do in her new backyard."

"The layout is pretty similar to yours. I am so excited. I can't believe we're going to be neighbors again!"

"You might not believe this, but no one is happier than me to have you both so close, especially during the holidays," DeeAnn said as she put an arm around each woman, "The holidays were always the loneliest time for me, especially after mom and dad died. I never thought I would have the chance to be a part of this family again."

"You were always a part of our family," Mary Elle said as she rested her head on her sister's shoulder.

"Even when you were a brat, we never stopped loving you," Rita said, giving DeeAnn a slight squeeze.

They stood in the backyard with their arms around each other for a few more minutes, enjoying each other's company. This moment was one that Mary Elle had always longed for. These women were her tribe. When everything else fell apart, she knew she would always have them; together, they could get through anything.

DeeAnn was the first to break away from their embrace. "So, Mary Elle?"

"Yes?"

"How's the wedding planning going?"

"Oh, I haven't even started. I'm sure it'll be a while before we get married." Mary Elle knew everyone would ask her about the wedding, and she dreaded it.

"Why? I thought you would be so excited to plan your wedding that you would get married in no time," Rita said with a confused look.

"Thomas and I aren't in a rush; things are great the way they are," Mary Elle said, hoping they could move on to a different topic of conversation.

She wasn't sure why she wasn't more excited about her wedding. She loved Thomas, she really did, and she knew he was the man she wanted to spend the rest of her life with. But she hadn't been divorced for very long. Was she ready to jump into marriage again? What if things changed once they married? A part of her knew it was silly to think like this, but she couldn't help herself and didn't want to mention it to anyone. She didn't have cold feet. She just wanted to enjoy life on her own for a little longer.

CHAPTER 2

"Honey, I'm home!" Rita called out as she walked into her home. The place was in complete disarray, with moving boxes everywhere. At the sound of her voice, Penny came running down the stairs.

"My sweet girl," Rita said as she picked her up, gave her a few kisses on her cute little face, and then sat her back down on the floor.

Penny stayed close by, wagging her little tail, probably waiting for a treat.

"Hi Honey, you're back early," Bob said as he walked in through the garage side door in their kitchen carrying some boxes. He gave her a quick peck on the cheek before setting the boxes on their kitchen island.

"What's all this?" Rita asked as she tried to peek inside the boxes.

"Just some tools I had in the garage. I'll be picking up a moving truck later today and want to load it up as much as possible."

"The boys said they would come by to help us move. I

don't want you overworking yourself, Robert," Rita said sternly.

She had to be stern. The man didn't know his limits.

The boys were her sister's kids. Rita's sister, Emma, had been a single mother from a very young age. Rita and Bob had taken custody of her three kids when her sister fell on hard times. It was that, or they would be placed in a foster home.

Bob and Rita didn't even need to discuss it. They said yes without a second thought. The oldest was Alexander. Last year, he married a lovely young lady named Caroline from South Carolina. Bob and Rita adored her. She had brought so much love and joy to Alexander's life. Alexander was a fantastic man who made them all proud of his accomplishments. But Rita always worried about him because she knew he had many emotions hidden inside that he never voiced to any of them. She hoped that he at least opened up to Caroline. It wasn't healthy for him to keep those feelings inside.

When Alexander was a young boy, he had been very quick-tempered and often got into trouble at school. As time went on, he calmed down. Rita and Bob had always made him feel loved and explained that there were other ways of expressing himself.

Then there was Andrew, who was single and was the same age as Michael, Mary Elle's son; the two boys are still very close. They went to the same school and played on the same sports teams. Unlike Michael, Andrew had stayed close to home in Atlanta. He went to Georgia Tech and graduated with an electrical engineering degree. He was working and continuing his education for his Ph.D. in Electrical and Computer Engineering.

The youngest was Amanda, Little Mandy Lou, as Bob called her. She had just turned 18 and started college. She was living in a dorm in Atlanta. Amanda wasn't sure what she would major in and only took the usual basic introductory courses.

"Stop worrying about me. I am fine," Bob said as he stood behind Rita and massaged her shoulders.

"Honey, you're not fine. The doctor said you need to take things slow," she reminded him.

Bob had been dealing with heart problems and had been in and out of the hospital a few times this past year.

"Okay, I'll slow down if you promise to stop worrying," Bob said, holding his hand out, signaling a truce.

"Okay, deal," Rita said and shook his hand on it.

She knew that she would never stop worrying about him no matter what. She only hoped the boys would get here soon.

* * *

"Knock knock!" Melanie said as she walked into her mother's office with baby Ryder asleep in his stroller. She hadn't noticed the older woman sitting in the office with her mom before it was too late.

"Melanie! I wasn't expecting you," Mary Elle said as she quickly jumped out of her seat and pulled her daughter into a warm embrace.

"I was getting a little stir-crazy at home, so I came to see if you wanted to have lunch with me," Melanie said.

She was still on maternity leave, and although she loved being a mom and spending time with her handsome boy, she had difficulty staying away from work. She was getting a little stir-crazy at home. In her first couple of weeks at home with Ryder, she had tackled doing little things around the house that were still pending while he slept.

"I'd love to. Let me introduce you to Mrs. Waskosky. She'll be working in the gift shop with Lisa."

Willow Acres had seen a steep increase in visitors that Lisa could no longer operate the bakery and gift shop by herself. It was a great problem to have.

"So nice to meet you," Melanie said as she extended her hand.

"I've heard so much about you from your mother. She just showed me pictures of your adorable little boy. You are so blessed!"

"Thank you, he is the greatest blessing," Melanie said as she glanced down to see Ryders' cute little face.

He was such a delightful baby. He wasn't fussy at all and loved to sleep.

"I will head back to the shop now. Enjoy your lunch, ladies," Mrs. Waskosky said as she left the room.

"She's so cute," Melanie said.

"She's great. A very hard worker and a quick learner. She's 73. Can you believe it?"

"No. She looks great. I hope I look like that when I'm her age."

"Me too. Her husband passed away recently, and Mrs. Adelman thought it would be a good idea to get her a job here."

"That's sweet. Being here and staying busy will help her deal with her loss. How is Mrs. Adelman? I haven't seen her around lately."

"She's doing well. The Inn has been keeping her busy, but she's still up to her old tricks," Mary Elle said with a smile.

Mrs. Adelman held a very special place in Mary Elle's heart. She owned the house next door to Mary Elle and took turns between staying there and at the Inn. Mrs. Adelman was in her 70s but worked harder than anyone Mary Elle knew.

She was getting older now and had hired help at the Inn, but unfortunately, the service was only temporary, as many couldn't keep up with the job's demands. Running an Inn wasn't for everyone.

"I made a scarf. I think she will love it. It has many funky colors. I need to remember to pass by the Inn to drop it off for her," Melanie said.

Melanie had taken up knitting while on maternity leave. Her first project had been to make little socks for Ryder. Now she knitted all the time and made different gifts for everyone.

"She would love that, and I'm sure she'd love to see little Ryder." Mary Elle said as she gently touched his face, careful not to wake him.

"Maybe I'll pass by later today. Are you ready for lunch? I heard Dean made cranberry pasta that I can't wait to try!"

Ryder stirred in his stroller, and Melanie bent down to soothe him. Mary Elle was so happy to see Melanie embracing motherhood the way she had. She had been so worried that she would fall into depression or it would be too much to handle, but she was a natural at it. Cade had also played a big part in that. He had helped Melanie in so many ways. From handling all the legal aspects of her divorce to helping remodel her new home and now just being there for her and baby Ryder. Mary Elle couldn't imagine a better man for her daughter.

* * *

RITA WAS EXTREMELY OVERWHELMED TRYING to pack everything up and constantly worried about Bob. She loved the man dearly, but he would give her heart problems. He was nonstop, wanting to do everything at once, even though the doctor told him he had to slow down.

Some months ago, he'd had an atrial fibrillation episode that scared Rita half to death. The doctor later told them he would lead a long life if managed correctly. He had a heart monitor that tracked his heart rate, but Rita still worried he was overexerting himself.

"Okay, where do I put this box?" Mary Elle asked as she walked out of the pantry closet.

Mary Elle and DeeAnn had known Rita was feeling overwhelmed and offered to help her pack. Rita appreciated their help more than they could ever imagine.

"Just place it by the door, and we'll move them to the moving truck later."

"Are you excited about the move?" DeeAnn asked her.

"I am. It's bittersweet. We made so many memories in this house, but I am looking forward to spending time with Robert and slowing down. He's always been on the go that I'm not sure how he'll handle retirement," Rita said with a laugh.

"Luckily, Willow Heights has a way of slowing everyone down naturally. It might take him a little while to adjust, but he'll learn to love it."

"You're right, though I'm sure he'll find something to keep himself busy. He's already talking about buying his antique dream car and fixing it up," Rita said with a slight shake of her head.

"That's not a bad idea. Thomas has been working on an antique tractor that his father left him. I'm sure this will be a bonding experience for them."

"Oh, I didn't know Thomas was into fixing antiques. I'll let Bob know."

"He is, and he knows where to find parts if Bob has difficulty finding them online."

"Oh, look at this. This is Alexander's old blankie. He loved this blanket so much and wouldn't sleep without it."

"Now that he's married, he can pass it on to his children," DeeAnn said.

"That's a lovely idea. How did they grow up so fast?"

"I'm not sure, but I love being a grandma!"

DeeAnn had been quiet. She was still single and without children. She was in her 40s and had been in relationships, but not in any serious relationships. The right guy just hadn't come into her life yet.

DeeAnn told them she knew God had someone special for her. She loved kids and always wanted to adopt if she couldn't have children. The ladies knew DeeAnn had been feeling down and tried to be there for her the best they could.

"I heard a new principal is coming to Willow Heights Middle school," Rita said as she noticed how quiet DeeAnn had become.

"Yes, he'll be here when classes start in January. Our old principal got sick and had to retire earlier than expected."

"Oh, is he from town?" Mary Elle asked as she lifted a box and placed it in the corner with the others.

"No, I heard he's from Atlanta, but they didn't mention any names."

"DeeAnn, didn't you date a principal back in Atlanta?" Mary Elle asked out of the blue.

"Yeah, I did, but things didn't work out. We had busy schedules. He was the principal of a high school, which was stressful for him. It just wasn't the right time for us, I guess." DeeAnn said.

"Don't worry, Dee, you're a great catch, and you deserve a great guy that will appreciate and love you," Rita said with certainty.

"It'll happen when it's meant to. All I have to do is trust in God's perfect timing," DeeAnn said with a sad smile.

Rita felt for DeeAnn; she truly deserved to find love and happiness. She wasn't sure why she hadn't yet. DeeAnn was intelligent and independent. She had traveled worldwide and done things Rita had only seen in movies or read about in books. She wondered if Bob might know someone they could introduce her to. Rita made a mental note to ask him soon.

* * *

THE LADIES TOOK a break from packing to do a little Christmas shopping. Some local shops in Willow Heights had different sales to kick off the holidays. They did this to bring more business into town and help small businesses that often suffered during the holidays when everyone went to more easily accessible chain stores.

It was early December, and the Christmas tree's annual lighting hadn't taken place yet. Mary Elle couldn't wait to see all wreaths on the light posts and the shops with their best Christmas lights and décor in their display windows. She remembered how much she loved it when she was a kid. The town was transformed and looked a lot like Christmas.

It was a unique experience here in a small town like Willow Heights. You could volunteer to decorate the main square. It was unlike in big cities where the streets are decorated overnight, and the residents don't participate. Here it was a family experience.

The ladies walked around the town square and discussed their plans for this year's Christmas party.

"With Christmas right around the corner, we haven't decided where we'll host our party." Mary Elle said.

"Well, Mary Elle, you being the party planner, I thought you had it all figured out," DeeAnn said with a sly smile.

"I haven't asked Thomas if we can host it at Willow Acres. I don't want to make anyone work for Christmas. But I would graciously accept helping hands." Mary Elle said, hinting at DeeAnn.

"Sign Bob and me up. I want to immerse myself in all things Willow Heights," Rita said as she bumped her hip with Mary Elle's.

The hip bump was much stronger than Rita planned, which caused Mary Elle to push DeeAnn onto an unsuspecting stranger.

"I am so sorry!" DeeAnn said as she brought her hands to her face in shame.

"It's okay. I didn't just pay $3 for this cup of coffee, and this isn't my favorite sweater," a very handsome man said with a smile.

"This is totally my fault!" Rita said as she dug around her purse for some napkins.

"It's okay. Please don't worry about it."

"Take this," DeeAnn said, handing him a ten-dollar bill.

"No," he said, shaking his head.

"Please, it's the least I can do. I feel awful. Use it to take your sweater to the dry cleaner and get yourself another cup of coffee," DeeAnn said, holding the money out.

"Honestly, it's fine. Enjoy the rest of your day, ladies," the handsome stranger said and quickly turned, getting lost in the crowd.

DeeAnn quickly spun to Mary Elle and Rita wide-eyed, and they broke into a fit of laughter.

"That was so embarrassing! What were you two thinking?" DeeAnn exclaimed.

"It was Rita's fault!" Mary Elle said, pointing at Rita the same way she had when they were kids and got caught doing something they weren't supposed to.

"He was good-looking, though, wasn't he?" Rita said with an evil laugh.

DeeAnn shook her head, and they continued on their way.

The first shop they visited was the Soapy Mitten. They

carried all kinds of natural handmade soaps for showers and had special bath bombs and loofas. The shop smelled divine.

Mary Elle bought Tiffany several little bath bombs and a lavender set that included the shower gel and oil-infused shower mittens. She bought Melanie a honeysuckle set with bath bombs and shower gels. For Michael, she picked out a sandalwood and vanilla set. Mary Elle figured it was manly yet sweet, just like her son. She got milk and honey soap for Thomas and a sandalwood hand soap for the office. She also snuck in some surprises for Rita, Bob, and DeeAnn.

After that, they visited a jewelry shop where the owner, Ms. Monroe, showed them how she made sterling silver rings and shared the shop's history. The shop had been in Willow Heights for many decades. The ladies bought several rings with stones as gifts, and Mary Elle fell in love with Opal silver earrings that she knew were perfect for Melanie. Melanie loved opals and iridescent things.

The next shop was a small art gallery. The owners, Matthew and his wife Sage, had their paintings on display. Sage's watercolors were beautiful, full of emotion, and told a story. Matthew's art is mixed media and uniquely captures his passion for nature and life.

Rita bought one of Matthew's art pieces for Andrew. DeeAnn bought two of Sage's watercolors and asked if they offered art classes for adults. Sage said they had been thinking about offering classes on the weekends and would let DeeAnn know when they would offer them.

DeeAnn loved learning new things. When they were small, their mother, Gladys, had paid for them to learn to play the piano. Mary Elle stuck to learning the piano; DeeAnn didn't like the piano and gave up and moved on to the guitar. DeeAnn enjoyed the guitar and learned to play well. In high school, DeeAnn learned German for fun. DeeAnn was excited to learn how to paint using watercolors.

An Amish couple owned the last shop they went to. Jacob and Miriam. The couple moved to Willow Heights and opened their shop in the 90s. They made clothing and shoes. They had the cutest little dresses for girls and outfits for boys. Ryder was getting a tiny suit for Christmas.

* * *

THEY MET at Rita's house again the next day to continue packing. They had enjoyed their little break yesterday and spent way more than they had planned, but they had a great time together. After packing up Rita's closet, they headed downstairs to where Bob was in the garage, moving some boxes.

"Alex, you came by to help us," Rita said when she saw him coming out of the garage with some boxes.

"Of course. How could I not help? Dad shouldn't stress, and neither should you."

Shortly after they took them in, the boys addressed them as mom and dad. Amanda was just a baby and couldn't even speak then. Hearing them call them mom and dad had touched Rita and Bob. They weren't planning on having their own kids and hearing them say that proved they made the right choice when they adopted them.

When they took in Emma's children, Mary Elle was there for Rita and taught her everything she knew about being a mother. Rita and Mary Elle raised their children together. They would often go on playdates with the kids, and, to this day, the kids were still very close.

"Miss Dee, one of my favorite teachers!" Alexander said when he spotted DeeAnn.

"Wow, I haven't seen you since you were in 5th grade, giving me a hard time at school!" DeeAnn said, laughing as she recalled the memory.

Alexander had been in DeeAnn's 5th-grade history class during her first year of teaching. He always played pranks on his classmates and had difficulty staying in his seat. Those days were a learning experience for DeeAnn as well.

"How are you feeling, Bob?" Mary Elle asked him. He was sneaking some beef jerky into the living room from the garage.

"I'm feeling great," Bob said as he discreetly put a piece of beef jerky in his mouth.

Rita noticed the beef jerky. "Having a late snack?"

"We've been working so hard. I got hungry. It's just a small piece; it won't do any harm."

"Oh, alright. But no more salty treats for you, Mister!"

Rita was always a softie for Bob. She loved him so much. They had been together for what seemed like a lifetime. He was her best friend, and they were inseparable, except for when Bob had to go out of town on business trips. Thankfully, that was in the past now.

When Rita and Bob started dating, Mary Elle had been the third wheel for most of high school. When Mary Elle started dating Bill, the two couples always went on double dates. That didn't last long because the two men didn't get along. Instead of forcing a friendship between the two, the ladies decided to let them be. At least their kids got along, and they all spent time together that way. Mary Elle's kids loved Bob and considered him an uncle. He missed none of their games or school dances. Growing up, he was there for them more than their father, even with his crazy travel schedule.

Mary Elle and DeeAnn left for the day, promising to be back tomorrow to continue packing. Rita went in search of her dear little Penny. She was probably sleeping in their bedroom. She loved sneaking in with her favorite toy and usually fell asleep under the bed.

"Where's my Penny Bear?" Rita called out. You could hear Penny's little paws against the wooden floor. It was as if she was running a marathon.

"There you are! My pretty girl! Oh, how I missed you!" Rita said as she rubbed her belly.

"Rita, you're never that sweet to me!" Bob called out from the living room.

"Oh, Bob, you silly old man," Rita said with a smile.

Bob was constantly telling her she spoiled Penny more than him.

Rita gave Penny some more belly rubs and kisses on her head before heading to the kitchen to serve Penny her dinner.

"Honey, we have to talk about the backyard in the new house. We need new plants, and it'll be relaxing for you," Rita said as she looked out the window. Their backyard in the new house was much bigger.

"Rita, it's winter. We can't start planting yet. We must wait until spring, but we can get some nice indoor plants. I was reading about the snake plant. It cleans the air. We should get some of those."

Because of Rita's love for plants, Bob had also gotten interested in them. When he was home, he would often help her with yard work on the weekends. Rita couldn't wait for them to get their hands dirty at their new home.

"We also haven't gotten our Christmas tree. You know it's our tradition to decorate the house and the tree with the kids. We should get it this weekend while the kids are visiting."

"Ok, honey. We will," Bob said, but he didn't sound like he was listening.

Alexander walked back inside with some firewood and started the chimney. He loved the smell of burning wood.

"I overheard we are decorating for Christmas this year. Is that right?" he asked.

"Yes, we are, and I'll make your favorite pecan pie," Rita said with a wink.

Alexander requested pecan pie every year without fail, and there was no way Rita would ever say no to him.

"I can't wait. This will be Caroline's first Christmas as Mrs. Holloway. I want to keep the same traditions as we have with you, mom."

After it had been clear that Emma wouldn't return, the social worker asked Bob and Rita if they would be open to officially adopting the kids. They sat down with the kids and asked them if they would want that. Alexander had broken down crying and said that was all he ever wanted. Now all these kids have their last name. Rita often wondered where her sister might be, but even with the help of private detectives, they never found her.

"Don't worry; I will remind her of your favorite Christmas traditions and ask if she has any traditions with her family," Rita said to him.

She knew how important it was for Alexander that Caroline felt welcomed into their life. Caroline also had a tough upbringing and wasn't very close to her family.

The doorbell rang, and Andrew walked in before they could see who it was. The kids all had keys to the house, but they still liked to announce their presence by ringing the doorbell before inviting themselves in.

"Andrew!" Rita said as she made her way over to him.

"Happy to see me?" He asked with a bright smile.

"We thought you weren't coming until the weekend. What a wonderful surprise." Rita said as she enveloped him in a big hug.

"I planned the surprise. I'm shocked Alex didn't tell you."

"There he is," Bob said as he greeted Andrew and patted him on the back.

"Hey, Dad, how are you?"

"Here, living and loving life. I got my boys and my lady with me; what else could I possibly need? This day couldn't get any better." Bob said as he slung an arm around Rita and Andrew. "Where's little Mandy Lou?"

"I told you. She's doing finals this week. She'll come home this weekend," Rita said.

They're interrupted by a knock on the door, and Alexander goes over to open it. Rita and Bob are waiting in anticipation. Who could it be?

"Hey! I wasn't expecting you!" Alexander said a little too loudly.

Bob and Rita looked at each other and then looked back at the doorway obscured by Alexander's body. Who could it be?

"Sorry guys, I forgot my phone," DeeAnn said as she poked her head out from Alexander's side.

Rita and Bob's faces looked confused and somewhat disappointed. They thought Amanda had surprised them by arriving tonight instead of the weekend.

"Oh, it's you," Rita said.

Alexander and Andrew laughed as they saw DeeAnn's confused face.

"I'm leaving now," she announced as she grabbed her phone and quickly made her way out.

"I thought it was Mandy," Rita said as she walked over to Alexander and gave him a light smack on the arm.

"What? It was funny."

Rita said nothing. She just shook her head with a smile on her face. No matter how old, these boys never stopped with their pranks.

CHAPTER 3

$\mathcal{M}$elanie stood at the sink, hand washing and drying the plates from her dinner with Cade. He came over after work, and they made spaghetti Bolognese together. Cade insisted they have garlic bread, salad, and a glass of sweet tea.

Mel's cooking skills were improving each day. When she lived in New York, she rarely ever cooked. Not because she didn't enjoy it, but because it only made her feel lonelier having to cook for one person.

Cade preferred home-cooked meals, though they went out on dates at least once a week. Melanie loved these sweet moments she got to share with Cade. After her experience in her first marriage with Everett, she never thought she would have this. Her relationship with Cade was one she had longed for since she was a young girl. She thanked God every day for bringing him into her life. He was sweet and thoughtful, and she had never seen him angry or in a bad mood.

"How are you feeling?" Cade asked as he came back inside from throwing the trash out.

"I'm a little tired, but we can watch a movie if you'd like," Melanie said, not ready for Cade to go home.

"Sure, those Christmas movies you love are out. We can watch one of those," he said with a playful groan as he made his way to the tv and searched for a movie.

Melanie loved sappy Christmas movies; she and Cade made a deal that they would take turns picking movies. Cade wasn't a fan of Christmas movies but loved Melanie, so he sat through them. Plus, they would watch one of his picks the next time, which were usually zombie-related or action-packed. He insisted he didn't enjoy watching the Christmas movies, but Melanie began to believe he was lying.

Melanie finished up in the kitchen and joined Cade in the living room. She brought her video baby monitor to watch Ryder while he slept in his nursery. Melanie checked the monitor and saw he was asleep in his crib with a little smile on his face.

"Your mom must be excited to have Rita move to Willow Heights," Cade said.

"Oh, they are like two little kids unattended in a candy shop. It's adorable."

All her mom and Rita talked about was the move, how they would decorate Rita's new home and everything they would do. Melanie was happy to have Rita and Bob join them in Willow Heights. Growing up, they were a constant fixture in her life, and it felt like coming full circle having them move here.

Rita was like a second mom to Melanie, and she valued her opinion a lot. She knew having Rita and Bob so far away had been hard on Mary Elle, though she never mentioned it. Her mother and Rita had been inseparable since they were kids, and the last year was the only time they had been apart. It didn't help that Uncle Bob started having heart issues, which put them all on very high alert.

Cade massaged Melanie's feet when he said, "I can't wait till we're married and get to do this every night."

Realizing what he'd just said, Melanie couldn't help but smile. "Married?" she asked with a raised brow.

"Yeah, I thought that was the path we were heading on," Cade said with a shrug of his shoulders as if what he said wasn't entirely monumental.

"Yeah, of course," Melanie said, unable to hide her smile.

Cade was thinking about marrying her! All she wanted to do was stand up and do a little happy dance, but he might think she was crazy if she did. So, instead, she planted a kiss on his cheek and snuggled in close.

* * *

"THIS IS OUR LOVELY CHRISTMAS VENUE," Mary Elle said as she opened the barn's doors for Rita and Bob.

Rita had confided that Bob had been in a rut since his retirement and needed something to keep him busy but safe. Mary Elle couldn't think of anything better to keep him busy than recruiting him for the Christmas party planning committee. It hadn't been what either Bob or Rita had in mind, but he was a good sport. Today they were touring the barn where they would host the Christmas party.

"This is a nice place," Bob said as he took in his surroundings.

"It looks so much more different from when I was here last," Rita said to Mary Elle.

The first time Rita visited Willow Acres, the barn had been in shambles and used for storage.

"David has been working very hard in the remodel and expansion. I often get lost because everything looks so different from one day to the next," Mary Elle said with a giggle.

Willow Acres has become a popular spot for those seeking a mountain getaway. The town was very family-friendly but also great for solo trips. There were plenty of things to do. A new business had opened up with zip-lining and other fun obstacle courses for adults and kids. The town also offered water tubing, horseback riding, and mini-golf, among other things. For lodging, the town had Mrs. Adelman's Inn, Cade's gorgeous A-frame cabins and Willow Acres would soon re-open their Inn.

"So, you said you need seating for this area?" Bob asked.

"Yes, for about thirty people. I was thinking of long wooden tables that could fit ten people, which would leave us enough space for a dance floor and food area," Mary Elle said as she motioned around with her hands where she envisioned each area.

"Seems like my retirement happened at just the right time. I will have those tables ready for you in no time. Do you need me to make you some chairs too?" Bob asked.

"I think making the tables should keep you busy for a while. I'll get the chairs elsewhere since we need them for Christmas."

"Sounds like a plan," Bob said and quickly headed to the work shed to look for supplies.

"Thank you so much for doing this," Rita said.

"You know there's nothing I wouldn't do for you and Bob. Also, have you seen all the furniture Bob has built in the past? You guys are doing me a favor," Mary Elle said.

From a young age, Bob had been into making furniture. When he and Rita wed, they didn't have much money, but Rita had fallen in love with a dining table that was three times their monthly mortgage. Bob surprised her a month later with the same table, except it wasn't the table from the store that would've cost them all their savings. He had made the table himself. As his career took off, his furniture-making stopped, so having him build these tables seemed like the perfect thing to get him back to his roots now that he had free time.

"And there's absolutely nothing we wouldn't do for you," Rita said as Mary Elle looped her arm with hers, and they made their way to the restaurant where Dean had made a delicious mac n cheese casserole with bits of ham that was calling their name.

* * *

As RITA WALKED into the house, Penny greeted her with a toy. "It's playtime. Let's go to the backyard, my little Penny bear," Rita said as she grabbed a couple of Penny's favorite balls to play fetch.

It had snowed lightly, and Penny wasn't sure what to make of it. She tried walking on the snowy grass but ran back inside and sat by the back door waiting for Rita to let her back in the house.

"You don't like the snow, Penny?" Rita said as she walked back inside the house. "Here, let's put on some little boots on you. Do you want a sweater too?"

Penny looked up at Rita, wagging her tail and jumping up and down.

"Rita, she's a dog," Bob called out from the living room, watching the news, "let Penny experience the snow."

She ran back inside; she needed her boots. "Don't you, Penny?" Rita asked the dog as she opened the linen closet used as Penny's closet. They filled it with all her little toys, treats, and clothes.

"Alexander left a voicemail. He's coming over tonight with Caroline," Bob called out.

"Ok, I'll start making dinner. What are you in the mood for, my love?"

"How about some beef stew or chili?"

"Great choices, dear; I think it's the perfect weather for chili."

"Call me when dinner's ready. I'm going to the garage to unpack some things; I need to find some tools to get started on the tables for Mary Elle."

"Sounds like a plan. Let me know if you need anything."

It felt great having Bob around the house now. He was usually at work or on business trips. The stress level was high, and it started affecting his heart. Retiring was the best decision for them, and it would give Bob a chance to relax and get back to being healthy. She could also monitor him and make sure he was eating right. Rita loved cooking and making everyone's favorite dishes. Now she could try out all her recipes on Bob. She knew Caroline loved her special chili, which was also Bob's favorite, so she got to work in the kitchen.

Alexander and Caroline arrived just in time. Rita had set the table for dinner and made some tea and hot chocolate in case they were in the mood. She knew Bob would want some hot chocolate.

"Hi there," Rita said as she opened the door for Alexander and Caroline.

"Wow, Rita, this house is so beautiful and perfect for you and Bob," Caroline said as she stepped inside and hugged Rita.

"Thanks, darling. We love it here."

"Where's dad?" Alexander asked.

"He's in the garage. I'll get him. Please make yourselves at home."

Rita went to get Bob and found him sitting with an old photo album.

"Bob, they are here, and dinner's ready," Rita said, interrupting whatever daydream Bob was having.

"Ok, honey, I'm going," Bob said as he stood and put the photo album away.

"It's so nice to have you visit us, Caroline," Rita said as she sat down a tray with mugs, "We have tea and hot chocolate."

"Thanks, Rita; you know I love white tea."

"I'll have hot chocolate with marshmallows," Alexander said with a big smile. Alexander had never outgrown his sweet tooth.

"Hi everybody," Bob said from behind Rita's loveseat, "I'll have some hot chocolate."

"Dad, it's so great to see you again. We brought you guys a housewarming gift," Alexander said as he handed a white gift box to Rita. Bob came over to see what was in the box.

Rita opened the gift box and found a Christmas ornament that said best grandparents.

"What? Oh, my goodness!" Rita said as she felt tears forming in her eyes before throwing her arms around Caroline.

"That's excellent news, Alex. I'm so happy for you. You're going to be a brilliant father." Bob says as his eyes fill up with tears, too. "And you're going to be the very best mom," he said to Caroline as he hugged her.

"This is the best news we've had for some time. I'm so happy," Rita says as she wipes the tears off her face.

"We weren't expecting this blessing, but God sent us the perfect Christmas news," Caroline said as she cradled her tiny baby bump.

They enjoyed their delicious dinner and sat around the table talking. Rita didn't think she would be a grandmother so soon, but she was overjoyed and couldn't wait to share the news with Mary Elle and DeeAnn. She watched as Alexander whispered something in Caroline's ear, which brought a smile to her face. It warmed Rita's heart to see them so happy and in love. Alexander was such a good person. Rita wished Emma could see how her kids had turned out. She would be so proud as well.

CHAPTER 4

$\mathscr{L}$ife in Willow Heights differed from life in Atlanta; with the slower pace, you could take your time to get ready and, as the saying goes, 'stop to smell the roses.' Bob was getting used to Willow Heights. He was already friends with Mr. Allen, their neighbor. Bob was the kind of guy that could talk to anyone about anything.

Everywhere Bob went, he made friends. It was no surprise to Rita that Bob and Mr. Allen were already planning fishing trips. Mr. Allen was a widower. His wife, Anita, died a few years ago, and he had been all alone as their kids had grown up and moved away from Willow Heights.

It was nice having Bob around and seeing him in a relaxed setting. Working and traveling around the country had taken a toll on him. The competition was high, and his former boss had high selling quotas that had become almost impossible to meet. Bob enjoyed meeting new people and traveling, but he knew it wasn't easy on Rita, who stayed home alone with Penny now that the kids were older.

Rita loved being creative and creating things with her hands. She loved plants and gardening, but she also loved water coloring and working with polymer and resin. Apart from how close it was to Mary Elle's house, they also picked it because it has a beautiful sunroom. Rita envisioned setting up a small studio for her art with a corner dedicated to her favorite indoor plants. Now that they were in Willow Heights, she planned to get her creativity flowing again.

Rita also loved talking to her plants. She'd once heard on a tv show that talking to plants helped them grow. Call her crazy, but she felt they flourished since she started talking to her plants. It had become therapeutic for her now that she was constantly worrying about Bob. She felt a deep connection to nature. Ever since she was a child, she loved climbing trees and planting flowers. Growing up, she and Mary Elle would often go back to the forests behind their houses and get lost for hours. Their dads eventually built them a tree-house; they hid their treasures and kept all their favorite toys there.

As Rita was getting some of her canvases out of boxes, she found a wooden piece with her name that Bob had given her when they were in high school from his wood-shop class. She took it out to polish the wood and spray paint it to display in her studio.

"Hey, Rita Margarita," a very familiar voice said. Rita Margarita was her childhood nickname. Rita wasn't sure who came up with it. Her father insisted he had come up with the nickname, but Mary Elle often took the credit for it.

"Hey, when did you get here? I didn't hear you come in." Rita said as she spotted Mary Elle.

"Just now, Bob was outside, and he let me in. So, what have you been up to?"

"Alexander and Caroline visited us yesterday, and guess what? We are going to be grandparents!"

"That's amazing! Congratulations! You're going to love being a grandmother." Mary Elle said as they hugged.

"Now, little Ryder will have cousins to play with."

"Oh, you remember how our kids used to play together all the time? Remember those drives down to Disney World with them? Boy, time flies by!"

"I know. We are so thrilled to become grandparents. I can't wait until we take the grandkids down to Disney World."

"You'll be driving us, Rita." Mary Elle said with a small laugh. Mary Elle hated driving exceptionally long distances.

"How's Michael doing? You said he was engaged."

"He's his father's son, always working. I haven't had time to speak with him lately. The girls haven't heard from him much, just a text here and there. I've told him to invite his fiancée for the Christmas party, but he said he wasn't sure she would be in town. She's a flight attendant."

"Oh, I see. I hope we get to meet her soon." Rita said as she continued unpacking.

"Tiffany is coming down this weekend. She said work has been very slow and has more free time," Mary Elle said as she grabbed a box and began helping Rita unpack.

"They grow up too fast. I still remember Tiffany playing with Mandy and going to swimming lessons."

"How's Mandy doing? How's her first semester in college?"

"It's been great so far. She's still undecided about her major, but that's ok. She still has time to figure things out and to discover herself."

Amanda was a bright girl, and Rita knew she would figure it out soon enough. She was young and still had time to decide what she wanted to do with the rest of her life.

"How did we get so lucky with our kids?"

"God blessed us with the best ones!" Rita said, trying not to show that she was getting teary-eyed.

It was great for Mary Elle and Rita to be close again. They

spent almost every day together decorating Rita's new house, shopping, and having coffee at the Busy Bee Coffee Shop.

Life was good for them; they also hosted dinners at each other's homes. Thomas and Bob were also building a solid relationship with each other. Thomas had been helping Bob find parts for his car rebuild, and Bob had invited Thomas to go ice fishing with Mr. Allen.

* * *

THOMAS HAD CLEARED out the rest of the barn, and with just a week left till the Christmas party, Mary Elle called a meeting with the "Party Planning Committee," as she liked to call them.

"Meeting is in session," Mary Elle said with a sly smile. She'd heard that line on many tv shows and movies and had always wanted to use it.

"First order of business," Rita said, trying hard to contain her laughter.

"Yes, the first order of business. Bob, are the tables done?"

"Yes, ma'am, they are complete," Bob said with pride.

"Excellent. Next order of business. Melanie, did you get the beverages and alcohol needed?"

"Yes, Cade and I have already received the order and have everything needed to create a minibar."

"Perfect. Thank you. Next, how are we on floral and decorations, Tiffany?"

"I have a floral shop with our order, and Patty has offered to help me with the flowers. I'm still working on some decorations."

"Thank you, Patty, for helping us. We are so blessed to have such amazing talent among us. I will help you with the decorations. Rita, are we good with the ingredients for the dishes?"

"Yes, we have everything. Dean and Lisa have offered to help us cook here for easy transport."

"That's amazing. Thank you, Dean and Lisa. The food will be buffet-style. I think we have everything ready for the party. Any suggestions or ideas or any comments are welcome and encouraged."

There was silence for a while until David mentioned music or DJ.

"David, thanks for reminding us about music. Do we know any DJs?"

"I could give it a try," David said. "I've been practicing, and I have a set."

"Ok, sounds great. David will DJ for us. Anything else?"

Mrs. Waskosky raised her hand. She had been sitting quietly in the corner, observing everyone. She wasn't usually the shy type, but Mary Elle knew she felt a little out of place since she was new to the crew.

"Yes, Mrs. Waskosky?

"I would like to plan a few Christmas games and contests."

"That's a wonderful idea! I can't believe we hadn't thought of that. Thank you, Mrs. Waskosky."

Mary Elle knew Mrs. Waskosky was just the person for that. As the Vice President of the bingo team, she couldn't think of anyone better to take on that task.

"Oh, I almost forgot, DeeAnn, have you picked out a tree yet?"

"No, but I will go to the tree farm this weekend with Tiffany."

"Great. Anything else?" Mary Elle asked as she glanced down at her notes to ensure she hadn't missed anything.

No one mentioned anything else.

"Meeting adjourned," Mary Elle said and lightly tapped the table with her makeshift gavel.

CHAPTER 5

"Now, this is what I call a Christmas tree," Tiffany said as she stood right in front of the tallest tree on the tree farm.

"I don't even think this tree fits in the barn, Tiff," DeeAnn said as she looked up at the tree. This was probably the tallest tree she'd ever seen.

DeeAnn never had an actual tree before. She rarely ever decorated for the holidays. After her parents passed away, she usually spent the holidays alone. To combat the loneliness, she usually planned a vacation during Christmas time.

"What about this one?" Tiffany said, now standing in front of a more reasonably sized tree.

"This might work," DeeAnn said.

"Are you okay, auntie D?" Tiffany asked.

"Yes, why?"

"You don't seem excited. It's Christmas. Christmas is the best time of the year! It's the happiest time of the year."

"It's just been a long time since I celebrated Christmas."

Tiffany nodded in understanding and gave her aunt a quick side hug.

"Have you found what you were looking for?" A man said from behind them.

As DeeAnn turned to see him, she recognized him as the man she had crashed into on the sidewalk.

He must've recognized her because he broke into a smile and said, "No coffee today," as he held his hands up.

"Very funny," DeeAnn said, but she couldn't help but smile along with him. He had a great smile.

"I still feel terrible about what happened."

"Please don't. Accidents happen all the time."

"So, women randomly bump into you and spill coffee all over you?"

"No. I can't say that happens regularly," he said, flashing her another brilliant smile.

Tiffany had been standing quietly next to DeeAnn, witnessing the interaction. DeeAnn had forgotten that she was standing there and was startled when Tiffany's cell phone rang. Tiffany excused herself, and DeeAnn stayed behind with the handsome stranger.

"I'm sorry I never caught your name?" he said.

"Oh, it's DeeAnn," she said as she extended her hand to him.

"Pleased to officially meet you, DeeAnn. My name is Paul, and I just took over this tree farm from my uncle," he said as he shook her hand.

"So, you're new around here?" DeeAnn asked.

"I grew up here but moved away, and now I'm back. I've never seen you before. I take it you're new around here?"

She explained to him that she had moved here recently and was working as a teacher at the middle school. Paul listened and asked questions, making DeeAnn feel like he cared about what she had to say.

"Okay, I'm ready to chop these trees down!" Tiffany said as she reappeared.

"That's the spirit," Paul said with a smile.

DeeAnn smiled too. His smile was contagious.

"My aunt has never cut down her own tree before. She's never even had a Christmas tree, so today is a very special day," Tiffany said to Paul as they walked down rows of trees.

"Really?" Paul asked with a shocked look on his face.

"I mean, I had one of those small trees from the dollar section at the store," DeeAnn said with a shrug of her shoulders.

Tiffany and Paul stared at her, completely appalled, making DeeAnn break into a full belly laugh.

"We need to make this right," Paul said.

"We do, we really do," Tiffany said as she nodded in agreement.

They were only there for one Christmas tree, but Tiffany insisted that the more trees, the merrier, and DeeAnn wouldn't fight that logic. She didn't want to seem like the grinch, not when Tiffany and Paul seemed to be Santa's most enthusiastic little elves. Paul helped them cut down the trees they wanted and promised to deliver them to Willow Acres the next day.

On the way back to Willow Acres in the car, Tiffany asked, "So what was that about Auntie D?"

"What was what?" DeeAnn asked, playing dumb.

"Where do you know Paul from?"

DeeAnn retold their first encounter, and Tiffany, the hopeless romantic she was, said, "So when's the date?"

"Date? He hasn't asked me out."

"Why don't you ask him out?" Tiffany asked, wiggling her brows.

"No way, he's the guy. Plus, I know nothing about him," DeeAnn said, hiding her blush.

"That's not true. You know his name is Paul. He owns a tree farm, and he likes coffee."

"Tiffany, don't be silly," DeeAnn said, waving her hand.

However, in her mind, she was considering it. What If she asked him out? It would be so nice to go out on a date. It had been a very long time since she'd been on one.

* * *

ALL I WANT *for Christmas* is you played on the store's speaker while Thomas and Mary Elle shopped. They met his sister for lunch at Winding Creek Ranch in a couple of hours. They stopped at a nearby shopping center to find her a gift.

"What about this?" Mary Elle asked, holding out a Christmas-themed heated blanket.

"That's nice, but I would like to keep looking," Thomas said as he approached the jewelry counter.

Mary Elle had never met his sister, and she did not know what to look for. She was usually very good at finding gifts, but Thomas had never spoken much about Vera. All Mary Elle knew about her was that she lived in Winding Creek and that, like their other siblings, she hadn't wanted to be part of running Willow Acres, leaving Thomas in charge of continuing the family legacy.

"What is Vera like?" Mary Elle asked.

"I don't know. She's just Vera," Thomas said with a shrug.

Mary Elle rolled her eyes and said, "My man of many words."

"Vera likes to read. She also likes to cook, and she loves horses."

"Okay, now we're getting somewhere," Mary Elle said.

Mary Elle found a few things she thought Vera would like and organized them nicely in a basket. She also found a cute Christmas card and wrote a sweet message from her and Thomas.

Once they finished shopping, they made their way to Winding Creek Ranch.

"I'm excited to see this place during Christmas time. It was breathtaking during Emily's wedding. I can't imagine how beautiful it must be now."

"George usually goes all out for the holidays. We should come by with everyone one night for their Christmas light show," Thomas said.

George was the owner of Winding Creek Ranch. He and his wife Beatrice ran the place with the help of their sons. As they took a tour of the ranch, Thomas told Mary Elle that he and George had gone way back. They had both grown up in Willow Heights, and their grandparents were longtime friends. His sister Vera had dated George once upon a time. David and George's daughter had dated throughout High School but broke it off before they went to different Universities. Unlike David, Lindsay never moved back home after finishing her degree.

Shortly after they arrived at the restaurant and were seated, Vera showed up. Thomas stood as soon as he saw her and pulled her into a deep embrace.

"Long time no see, Thomas," Vera said.

"Vera, this is my fiancée, Mary Elle." Thomas said, placing his hand on Mary Elle's lower back.

They finished their introductions and took their seats. The server brought took their order, and they caught up.

"So, when is the wedding?" Vera asked.

"Soon," Thomas said.

"We're not in a rush," Mary Elle said simultaneously.

Thomas was surprised by Mary Elle's response and glanced at her with a confused look. They hadn't spoken about the wedding since the engagement. They had been too busy at Willow Acres hosting many holiday parties since they'd barely had a moment to process their engagement.

Mary Elle was quiet for the rest of the meal. Vera was friendly and asked her many questions, but Mary Elle wasn't as engaging as usual. She felt like she and Thomas weren't on the same page for the first time, and she didn't know what to think about that.

On the drive back home, Mary Elle was still quiet. She didn't know why she was still hesitating. She wanted to be with Thomas. Mary Elle loved him and knew he was nothing like Bill, so why was she holding herself back?

"Is everything ok, Elle?"

"Yes, everything is fine."

"Then why are you so quiet tonight? Did I do something wrong?" Thomas asked, squeezing her hand.

"No, honey. You have done nothing wrong. We haven't discussed the wedding, and I feel we're not on the same page."

"I love you, and you're the woman I see by my side every day for the rest of my life. Do you not feel the same way?"

"Of course I do. I love you, Thomas," she said.

"I know what I want, and I would rather start waking up by your side every day, sooner rather than later," Thomas said, squeezing her hand.

"But I just got out of a divorce. This is the first time I've ever been alone. I thought I would have more time to enjoy it," Mary Elle said, hating how she sounded.

"I see," Thomas said as his hand gripped the steering wheel and his eyes focused on the road ahead.

Mary Elle felt terrible about having conflicting emotions. Why couldn't relationships be easier? Why couldn't anyone understand where she was coming from? Wanting to wait for the wedding didn't mean she didn't love Thomas or was unsure of their future.

"Darling, I didn't know you felt that way. I love you as much, if not more now than before. I'm excited about the wedding and thought you'd like us to marry sooner rather than later. I'm certain you're the one I want to spend my days with," Thomas said, breaking the silence.

Mary Elle didn't know what to say. She held his hand a little tighter and looked out the window. They loved each other; they would work it out. There is absolutely nothing wrong with their relationship or wanting more time. Was there?

* * *

Rita had finished unpacking everything, and Bob had hung up the last photo frame in the hallway. The house was cozy, and it was perfect for them. Andrew had come over earlier and helped chop firewood for the chimney. It was cold, but the snow was not much and melted within a few hours.

"I love the smell of firewood burning in the chimney," Bob said as he placed wood pieces into the chimney, and Rita came to sit on their sofa with Penny.

"It's wonderful, Bob. Sit next to us. I made you some tea."

"Thanks, honey. You always spoil me," Bob said as he grabbed the mug and the tv remote.

"What are we watching?"

"I don't know. Want to watch a movie?"

"Which one is on?" Rita asked as Bob flipped through the channels.

"A body has been found on an abandoned back road that connects Willow Heights to Winding Creek. Officials have not identified the body found, but the medical examiner's office was seen taking the deceased person for identification. The cause of death has not been revealed yet. Stay tuned for more," the news anchor said.

"Wow, I never thought we would hear of murders or

anything like that here in Willow Heights," Rita said, feeling uneasy, and a chill went down her spine.

"Better lock our doors from now on," Bob commented.

"I hope they identify the person and find the killer soon."

"Me too," Bob said as he put an arm around Rita, and she snuggled in closer to his chest, her favorite place to be even after all these years.

* * *

Mary Elle and Tiffany sat at her dining table doing their nails. Tiffany purchased a gel nail kit and did Mary Elle's nails first.

"I saw this girl online who had this nail kit and ordered it. It was only 20 bucks, and it got here the next day. Isn't that awesome?" Tiffany said as she slowly painted the nail polish over her mother's fingers.

Once she finished that layer, Mary Elle would have to insert her hands into the UV light lamp to cure the polish.

"So, how long will this polish last?" Mary Elle asked as she put her hands in and felt the UV warming her hands.

"It should last a week or two. Sometimes even longer. It's still better than going to get our nails done. Do you know how many times I paid like 40 dollars only to walk out and ruin a nail?" Tiffany asked in that dramatic voice she used when trying to make a point.

"For 20 dollars, this isn't a terrible deal," Mary Elle commented.

Mary Elle loved getting her nails done and would take the girls with her to get manicures when they were little. They loved having girls' days where they could do all the girly things they loved. Whenever they had a girl's day, Mary Elle would have to plan a day to go out with Michael and do the things he enjoyed, like going to the arcade or the movies.

As Tiffany moved on to her mother's other hand, she admired her engagement ring.

"Thomas did very well with this ring," Tiffany commented.

"He did. I love it," Mary Elle said as she glanced at it.

It was a solitaire diamond ring. It was simple and elegant. Bill had given her a very ostentatious ring that had never been her style.

"Did he tell you he called me to ask me your ring size?"

"He did?" Mary Elle asked. Thomas hadn't mentioned it to her.

"He did. I guess I'm his favorite stepchild. You would think that he would've asked Melanie, but no, he asked little Ol' me," Tiffany said with a silly laugh.

"When is the wedding? I need to request that day off from work."

"I'm not sure yet. We haven't discussed it yet."

"Oh, okay," Tiffany said.

Mary Elle knew Tiffany wanted to know why, but she didn't press her. Mary Elle loved how close her kids and Thomas had become. They shared a great relationship. She figured it was because Thomas was so open and easygoing, and her kids responded to that. It also helped a lot that Thomas was supportive and loving towards her. The girls especially noticed and often commented on it, which was precisely why she wasn't sure she was holding herself back. What was wrong with her?

* * *

RITA SAT on her yoga mat in the lotus pose in her sunroom to clear her mind.

Bob walked in and asked, "Rita, why are you bending like a pretzel?"

Rita didn't want to lose her focus, but she couldn't help but laugh.

The birds were happily chirping in the trees nearby. She took a deep breath and tried to calm her nerves. Bob's heart monitor had been going off all morning.

They had called his doctor, but he said he was monitoring it and was okay. Rita didn't like this one bit. She wished there was something she could do to make Bob all better again. She didn't know what she would do if anything ever happened to him.

Penny came over, plopped herself on the yoga mat right in front of Rita, and dropped her slobber-filled ball right in front of her. When Rita didn't react, the dog nudged her hand and looked at the ball expectantly.

"Here you go, girl," Rita said as she gently tossed the ball as far as she could, hoping not to knock anything over.

Penny's veterinarian, Doctor Luke, suggested that Penny goes on a strict diet and for Rita to take her on walks to get some much-needed exercise. Penny was quickly getting her workout done every day and had already lost one pound, but Rita still found it hard to refuse her any treats. The dog knew exactly how to play at her heartstrings. Penny reappeared in front of Rita with the ball again, and they continued to toss and fetch for a few more minutes.

"Rita!" she heard her friend Mary Elle call from inside the house. "I'm in the sunroom," she called out as Mary Elle held a pitcher and a bag filled with Tupperware and began unloading everything on the table.

"What's all this?" Rita asked as she approached the table at the same time as Penny, sniffing the air and wagging her tail.

Penny let out a small woof and scratched at Mary Elle's leg in case she hadn't noticed her. Mary Elle bent down and scratched Penny behind the ear while giving her a dog treat when Rita wasn't looking.

"I brought some breakfast. I couldn't sleep, so I got up early and started baking and cooking. Have a seat, and let's dig in. I also squeezed the orange juice myself."

"Mary Elle, everything looks amazing, but you really shouldn't be worrying about me. Everything is under control." Rita hated being a burden to her friend.

She also hated that she couldn't stop worrying about Bob. Rita had never been much of a worrier. She usually left all her cares to the Lord, and she knew he would handle it, but this was Bob's heart they were dealing with. How could she not worry?

Recently, Mary Elle had been dealt a tough hand when she found out her husband was leaving her for none other than the town gossip and Mary Elle's childhood revival. Thankfully, Mary Elle had risen above it; she started by moving away from the never-ending gossip and people that wished her unwell. She got a great job and a second chance at love.

Mary Elle had come a long way, and Rita was proud of her friend's tenacity and willingness to forgive. Instead of wallowing in self-pity, she had lived her life on her terms. She had dedicated most of her life to her husband and kids, and now she was glowing with her newfound happiness. Rita didn't want to be the one to bring her spirits down.

"Worrying? No one is worrying," Mary Elle said with a wave of her hand. "I am simply using you as a taste tester."

"Taste tester?"

"You heard that right. I found this new cooking show, and I love all the recipes. I haven't been able to stop myself from trying them all."

"How do you have time for so much cooking when you're in your busiest season at work?"

"Honestly, I'm in over my head. I have three events scheduled for this weekend, and I still haven't had time to hire help."

"Is that your way of getting me to offer to help?" Rita asked with an amused smile.

She knew Mary Elle would do anything to get her out of the house to keep her from worrying about Bill.

"I'll gladly accept your help if you insist!" Mary Elle said, giggling.

Rita rolled her eyes and smiled. "You've never been good at being sneaky. Sure, I'll come help."

"Great! Phew, I just got a big load off my plate."

As they enjoyed their breakfast, they reflected on some old memories.

"Remember when Bob wanted to surprise you with breakfast in bed?" Mary Elle asked.

"How could I forget? He almost gave me salmonella!" Rita said with a laugh.

"He forgot to turn on the stove to make the eggs, and it didn't help that you told him you didn't like your eggs dry," Mary Elle said, giggling as she remembered how Rita had called her while hiding in her bathroom because she didn't know what to do and she didn't want to hurt his feelings.

"Mary Elle, are you making fun of my cooking skills in my home?" Bob asked as he appeared in the sunroom.

"Making fun? No way. I simply reminded Rita how much you love her and that you tried to make her eggs, though you had probably never set foot in a kitchen before."

"Well, that is true. There's nothing I wouldn't do for my lady," Bob said, kissing Rita on the top of her head before continuing with his day.

"So, I think Thomas is upset at me," Mary Elle said once Bob was out of earshot.

"Why?"

"I think he wants to get married soon, but I would like to wait longer."

"Why don't you want to get married soon? What's holding you back?" Rita asked.

She was genuinely confused about why Mary Elle was hesitating to marry Thomas. They were great together, and Rita had never seen Mary Elle happier than she was now.

"I don't know, Rita. Honestly, I don't know. I just got divorced recently. I love the way things are. Why change anything?"

CHAPTER 6

Alexander and his wife, Caroline, arrived early and brought Rita a new cactus. Andrew was coming later, and Amanda called to say she was driving over for dinner and would be there soon. The kids tried keeping her company while Bob was in the hospital. Rita didn't think it was fair for them to go out of their way to be there for her. She was fine. She just needed a little more time to process everything.

Bob's heart had been acting erratically, and when he went to get it checked out, they found out he had a blood clot. He needed to have it removed. The surgery was supposed to be easy, and he should've been home now, but they'd run into some complications, and he had to stay in the hospital a little longer.

She hated being so far away from him. Rita loved that they had their home in Willow Heights now, but they hadn't thoroughly thought it through when they decided to move to a tiny town without a hospital in the middle of dealing with Bob's heart issues. She went every day for visiting hours, but it wasn't enough time. She missed him.

Alexander gave Rita a quick hug before heading out to the grill. He had brought some salmon wrapped in foil to grill. Rita knew he had done it because that was her favorite. Since a young age, Alexander has always been very thoughtful and perceptive of others' needs. Both boys had always been very selfless growing up. Mandy had always been a little spoiled as the youngest and the only girl. It didn't help that Robert always covered for her when she did something she wasn't supposed to. Like breaking her brothers' toys or stealing their candy. She had been hard to tame from a very young age.

"How have you been holding up?" Caroline asked as she pulled Rita into a hug.

"I've been better. How are you and Alexander doing?" Rita asked as she gently pressed a hand on Caroline's belly.

"We're okay. Alexander has been working very long hours lately, but other than that, things are good. He's been worried about Bob, and I think working keeps him busy, so he prefers to spend his time there for now."

Andrew and Amanda arrived shortly after, and they spent the dinner recalling their favorite memories of growing up. Rita could tell they worried about Robert just as much as she did. She loved listening to them talk about Bob and hearing different stories they had about him she'd never heard before.

"Remember that teal vase Mary Elle gave you for one of your birthdays?" Andrew asked Rita.

"Yeah?" Rita said, unsure of where he was going with this.

"Well, this one time, Mandy and I were playing soccer in the living room and broke it," Andrew said, looking over to his sister.

Mandy covered her face and said, "I had forgotten about that! It smashed into a million little pieces."

"It did," Andrew continued, "We tried gluing them all

together and put it back where it was, but dad noticed and took us in search of a new one before you noticed."

"I knew the vase looked different! I mentioned it to him, and he assured me I was confused. I can't believe him!" Rita began laughing as she recalled that moment.

Oh, Bob, her silly man. How she missed him. He should be here with them instead of alone in a hospital room.

They continued eating their dinner and sharing funny stories. The kids brought Rita so much joy. Rita had learned that the most important and precious things were the little things in life, like spending time with your loved ones, enjoying a beautiful sunset, cuddling with your pet, and enjoying a delicious meal with great friends and family.

* * *

MARY ELLE WAS CRAWLING on her knees when she heard a knock on the door. She had been running around all day preparing for the three events. Rita oversaw the retirement party being held in the restaurant in Willow Acres. Melanie was at the barn overlooking a corporate dinner, and Mary Elle was getting everything together for tonight's wedding at the main house in Willow Acres.

She'd been carrying boxes with the silverware when the top box fell, and the silverware had flown everywhere. She was glad today's events were all being held at Willow Acres. Mary Elle didn't know what she would do if all three were at different venues. This way, she was close enough to prevent any fires.

There was a soft knock, and Mary Elle called out, "Come in!" hoping it was Mrs. Adelman's niece. She was supposed to be here two hours ago.

A young lady walked in and smiled apologetically when

she noticed Mary Elle struggling to keep the boxes together again.

"Do you need help?" she asked,

"Oh, thank God you're here! I was worried you would be a no-show. Mrs. Adelman said you'd be here about two hours ago. No worries, though; I am just glad you made it!" Mary Elle said as she handed her the boxes she'd been carrying.

"Actually..." the young lady began to say, but David and Cade walked in before she could say anything else.

"Thomas said you might need some help," David said,

"Yes! Thank you so much for coming. This is..." Mary Elle trailed off as she gestured towards the very confused-looking girl.

"Sienna," she said.

"Sienna. She'll be helping us today as well. We just need to get the rest of these boxes to the reception over at the ball-room to finish setting up for the wedding reception."

* * *

MARY ELLE WANTED nothing more than to jump into a warm bath at the end of the night. Tonight had been a success. Very stressful but successful. Her clients had all been satisfied with her services and mentioned booking her again for future events. She was truly blessed to have such a close-knit support team. They had all been able to work in perfect synchrony together. Even Sienna had fit right into their dynamic.

"Thanks so much for coming today," Mary Elle said to Sienna as she was about to walk out the door. "Please don't leave; I still need to pay you."

"Don't worry about it," Sienna said.

"You earned it! Just give me a moment, please." Mary Elle said as she searched for the check in her purse.

"Mary Elle, I'm not who you think I am."

"What do you mean?" Mary Elle asked as she stopped digging around in her purse and focused her attention on Sienna.

"I came by because I was looking for my parents. You seemed overwhelmed, and that's why I stayed and helped."

"Oh, my! I am so sorry. I was waiting for someone all day, and when you showed up, I assumed you were her," Mary Elle felt her cheeks flush.

She was so embarrassed. She had made this poor sweet girl do all this work when she was simply looking for someone.

"It's okay. Please don't apologize. I ended up having a great time with you all. It hardly felt like work."

"That's so sweet of you. Maybe I can help you. What is the name of the person you're looking for?"

"I'm looking for my birth parents, Rita and Robert Holloway."

"Rita." Mary Elle said in disbelief just as Rita was passing by.

"Did someone call me?" Rita asked, joining them.

"Hi," Sienna said and looked to Mary Elle for support, but Mary Elle was too confused to say anything.

"Hi," Rita replied with a smile.

"I think there's been a misunderstanding here," Mary Elle said.

"What do you mean?" Rita asked, looking from Mary Elle to Sienna, confused.

"Are you Rita Holloway?"

"Yes, I am. Why?"

"You're my birth mother," Sienna said.

Rita let out a gasp, and tears sprang to her eyes.

"Rita, is this true?" Mary Elle asked.

Rita didn't speak and simply nodded.

"How?" Mary Elle asked.

She'd known Rita her whole life. How could this be? How could she have never known? While speaking to Sienna earlier during the wedding reception, she knew she was two years older than Michael. That would mean Rita had her when she was 17.

* * *

"Wow, you're so beautiful," Rita said, looking intensely at Sienna's face. Rita felt like she was in a dream. How could this be happening? She couldn't help but pull Sienna into a deep embrace.

She looked just like Robert. This made Rita even more emotional. She hugged her again and sobbed. Sienna didn't say anything; she just let her hold her.

There was so much Rita wanted to say and explain to both Sienna and Mary Elle, but she didn't know where to start. She had dreamt of this moment many times before but always imagined Bob being by her side.

Although Bob and Rita have been married for about 25 years, they had also been high school sweethearts, and there was a lot to their story that many didn't know about.

"How did you find me?" Rita asked Sienna.

"I found my adoption papers a few years ago, and my mother explained everything. I know you had no choice but to give me up."

Suddenly, all the painful memories came back to Rita. Her parents found out she was pregnant the summer before her senior year. They sent her away to hide the pregnancy and prohibited her from telling anyone. Bob's parents had been in on the agreement.

Rita's parents found the family they gave the baby to. They had been in their mid-twenties and hadn't been able to conceive. They promised to provide the baby with the best life they could offer her.

Rita has never erased the memory from her mind of holding her baby after just giving birth and quickly having to hand her over and never seeing her again.

This had utterly torn Rita and Bob up. They never got over the guilt of having to give their baby away, and because of this, they had chosen not to birth any more kids. She had been so ashamed that she never even mentioned it to Mary Elle.

"Your father loves you so much. I wish he were here to see you now." Rita said.

"When I went to look for you at your last house, the person who answered told me he was recently hospitalized. They told me to come here to look for you. I didn't tell them I was your daughter, only that I was related to an old friend."

"I appreciate you coming and for being so understanding."

Bob and Rita had often wondered what had happened to that baby. They had to give up. He, too, loved the baby and always talked about her and imagined what her life would've been like.

Bob had been Rita's rock when she felt the pain of not having her in their lives and when doubt and guilt had crept in to question her decision and ability to be a mother. Bob was there through it all, with all his love. She couldn't wait to take Sienna to see him.

Rita introduced Sienna to Melanie, who was still in shock as well. No one knew about Rita's pregnancy or story.

"We are so happy to meet you!" Melanie said.

Thomas and the rest of the gang introduced themselves and thanked her for the help she had provided them in tonight's event. Rita loved seeing her daughter bonding with all those closest to her. It gave her hope that they could finally have a relationship with each other after all these years.

Mary Elle got in the hug action as well; she loved hugs. She always said that a hug and a laugh cured everything.

"What other secrets do you have, Rita?" Mary Elle said, winking at Rita.

"She's my only secret. I'm so happy she is here. She's even more than I could have ever imagined her."

"Go catch up with her, Rita. We'll finish up the event. She's here for you. Don't waste any more time apart," Mary Elle said, squeezing Rita's shoulder.

"Thank you, Mary Elle. This has been the best night of my life. I can't believe she's here. I feel like this is a dream, and I'll wake up, and she'll be gone again."

"It's not a dream, Rita. She's here," Mary Elle said, hugging Rita.

* * *

As RITA and Sienna drove back home, they stopped to get some fast food on their way. Rita was over the moon. They ordered burgers, fries, and, of course, sweet tea for each.

"Sienna, where did you grow up?"

"I grew up in Virginia."

"I've been there; it's beautiful."

"Yes, my parents moved there when I was in middle school. Before that, we lived in Hilton Head, but mom and dad moved north to be closer to family."

"Oh, I see. Do you have siblings?"

"Yes, I have a younger sister. Her name is Olivia. She's also adopted. When I discovered those adoption documents, it changed many things in our family, as you can imagine. I never knew I wasn't their biological child and that Olivia wasn't my sister. They always treated me with lots of love.

They never made me feel less than or that I didn't belong. I had seen photos of me as a baby with them, so there were never any doubts, although now, thinking about it, there weren't any photos of my mom pregnant. I'm sorry I don't mean to offend you by calling her mom." Sienna said apologetically.

"It's ok; I have no problem with you calling her mom. She raised you; therefore, she is your mom. I'm just grateful they were loving and caring towards you. They raised you right. Look at how wonderful you are. I'm grateful they loved you so much."

"They did. They taught me well. I finished high school with excellent grades and a full-ride scholarship. They taught me the love of God. I'm grateful for all they did for me. I know they kept this from me not to make me feel bad. They told me you and Bob loved me and wanted the best for me. I know you wouldn't have given me up if you had the support and resources to raise a baby at such a young age."

"Thank you for understanding. You have no idea how much we love you. It was extremely difficult for us. It's been haunting me since you were born. We always thought about you and prayed that God led and protected you. We never had other children, we had you, and you were the fruit of our love. I'm happy beyond words and can't tell you how much happiness you've brought into my life. I never thought this day would come."

"Neither did I. I would love to hear more about my father. He sounds like an amazing husband, and I know he would've been an excellent father."

"Your father is in the hospital right now. He had a blood clot removed and hasn't been discharged yet. It's too late tonight to visit him, but we can go tomorrow. He would love to meet you."

"I can't wait."

* * *

Tiffany signed up to volunteer with the decorations in the town's square. She'd overheard Mrs. Adelman talking about it and had signed up right away. She has always dreamt of taking part in something like this.

"Do you think you can hang these wreaths on the benches, dear?" Mrs. Adelman asked.

"Of course!" Tiffany said as she eagerly took the wreaths from her.

About 20-30 people had shown up to help decorate today. They were putting twinkling white lights on all the trees. They were also hanging some that looked like ornaments and some that looked like cascading snowflakes.

Tiffany couldn't wait to see the finished product. It wouldn't be long until they had their annual Christmas tree lighting. The shops also decorated their windows, and everyone came to check them out. The Busy Bee Coffee shop also gave free hot chocolate and warm apple cider.

"You remind me so much of your grandmother," Mrs. Adelman said as she tied a red bow around a pole.

"I do?" Tiffany asked. She hadn't known her grandmother very well. Her grandmother passed away when Tiffany was very young.

"Oh yes. She loved Christmas, just like you. Gladys would drag your grandfather here every Christmas. She said it wasn't Christmas unless she was in Willow Heights. She was always the first to sign up to decorate the square."

"I wish I could remember her. When she passed away, I was very young. I have one very vivid memory of her giving me my favorite teddy bear. He's probably in my mom's basement somewhere."

"I wish she could see you all here now. Her girls are finally back together after all this time. To see you and

Melanie all grown up and little Ryder. Her heart would burst with joy."

"Hello, ladies," David said as he appeared next to them with a big box full of Christmas decorations.

"Good morning, my sweet boy," Mrs. Adelman said, giving him a peck on the cheek, leaving an imprint on his cheeks with her bright red lipstick.

"Hi, David," Tiffany said as she hung the wreaths.

"I didn't know you were in town," he said as he helped her.

"Yeah, I was in charge of the vital task of picking out the Christmas trees for the party. I had the weekend off from work, so I drove down."

"Trees? I thought it was just one?"

"Where's your Christmas spirit, David?" Tiffany asked as she bumped her shoulder with his.

David laughed and said, "I can't wait to see how it turns out," before he rushed over to help Mrs. Adelman, who seemed to struggle with some Christmas lights.

* * *

Mrs. Waskosky and Mrs. Adelman were having lunch by the lake when Mary Elle approached them. Mrs. Adelman had her hair up and was wearing her signature red lipstick.

"Hello, ladies; how are you all doing?" Mary Elle asked as she kissed each lady on the cheek.

"It's so good to see you, dear. Sit with us," Mrs. Adelman said.

"I was on my way to meet with Jasper and Patty, but I can chat for a bit," Mary Elle said as she sat down with them.

"I feel like I haven't seen you in months! I heard from Waskosky that you got engaged," Mrs. Adelman said with a disapproving glare.

"You know how she feels about not being one of the first in the know," Mrs. Waskosky said with a laugh.

Mrs. Adelman had a reputation for always knowing the comings and goings of everyone in town. She said it wasn't because she liked to gossip but that she just couldn't help always looking out for everyone. She deemed herself the town's official grandma. Her intentions were pure, so no one seemed to mind.

"I am so sorry. Things have been hectic, and I haven't had time to pass by the Inn. How about I call you and set a lunch date to catch up?"

"That would be very nice," Mrs. Adelman said.

"Is that the scarf Melanie knit for you?" Mary Elle asked when she noticed the gorgeous, colorful scarf around her neck.

Mrs. Adelman brought her hand to her neck and smiled, "Why yes, it is. She came by the Inn with little Ryder. He is such a cute chunky baby! He didn't even cry once the whole time they were there."

"He truly is the best baby," Mary Elle said as she pulled her phone out and shared pictures of baby Ryder.

"Melanie looks so much happier now. Cade is such a good match for her. I also volunteered with Tiffany earlier today at the square. She's such a sweet, bright girl," Mrs. Adelman said.

"I can't believe how grown my kids are. I feel like they were running around pulling each other's hair only yesterday. Now I'm a grandmother," Mary Elle said and felt tears forming in her eyes.

"They might've outgrown your lap but never your heart, and no matter what, they will always need you," Mrs. Waskosky said as she placed a hand over Mary Elle's.

CHAPTER 7

"This here is your ten Christmas trees," Paul said as he set the last tree down.

"What in the world am I supposed to do with all these trees?" DeeAnn asked as she stared at them, unsure what Tiffany had been thinking.

"Do you want me to help you set them up?" Paul asked as he shielded his eyes from the sun.

"Tiffany should be here to help me, but I'm not sure where she is, and she's not answering her phone, which is very unlike her," she said as she slipped her phone out of her pocket to see if maybe there was a notification she had missed.

"I'm free for the rest of the day. I don't mind helping you."

"Okay, let's get started," DeeAnn said, springing into action. If Tiffany would not show up, she might as well accept his help. Otherwise, she would be here all day.

They spent the next couple of hours setting up the trees in different areas around the farm. They placed one in the main lobby, one inside the barn where the Christmas party would be, and one outside the barn. DeeAnn and Paul also set one up in the restaurant, and any other place they thought might fit. When they were finally done, Tiffany showed up.

"Where have you been?" DeeAnn asked as she saw her approaching them.

"I'm so sorry. I had to watch Ryder, and I didn't have cell-phone service. Melanie hasn't set up a landline at home yet."

"I'm just glad you're okay. I was worrying."

"I see you found help," Tiffany said with a wide smile.

"Oh, him?" DeeAnn said as she looked over at Paul.

He was distracted playing with the new puppy at Willow Acres that Jasper found abandoned on the side of the road. He was so cute. Paul must have sensed them watching him because he looked up, and his eyes locked with DeeAnn's.

"Tiffany, you made it," he said as he jogged over to them.

"Thank you for helping my aunt. I'm sorry you got stuck doing my job. The Christmas Party planning committee would love to invite you to our annual Christmas party to pay you back for your trouble," Tiffany said.

"Count me in," he said before turning to DeeAnn and saying, "I had a great time. I hope I get to see you again soon."

"I'd like that," DeeAnn said as she stood there with Tiffany, watching him walk to his car.

"He's cute," Tiffany said, nudging DeeAnn with her elbow.

"Yes, he's also smart, funny, and totally out of my league."

"What? No way! You're gorgeous, and he would be lucky to score a date with you!"

"Thanks, Tiff," DeeAnn said.

DeeAnn had never been one to have low self-esteem, but things had been rough lately. Her last relationship ended when she caught her Ex-boyfriend with a supposed friend. She had never been cheated on before, and it messed with her head.

* * *

RITA AND SIENNA had breakfast together at the Busy Bee Coffee Shop. Once they finished, they went to Atlanta to visit Bob at the hospital. Rita didn't know how to tell Bob about Sienna, but she knew this would also lift a burden off of him. It has been difficult for both of them to keep this secret. They considered hiring a PI to help them find the baby, but they decided against it.

"Good morning, honey. How are you feeling today?" Rita asked as she walked into his room alone while Sienna waited outside.

"Hi darling, I'm ok. They just brought me breakfast," Bob said as he wiped his face.

"I have a surprise for you," Rita said, unable to contain her excitement.

"What is it?" Bob said, sitting up now. He loved surprises.

"Wait, I'll go get it. I left it at the door."

"I hope it's not another corgi," Bob said, laughing, but Rita knew he was hoping it wasn't another dog.

Rita came back in, with Sienna trailing close behind her. His eyes widened as he took Sienna in.

"Is that her?" Bob said, looking at Rita and then at Sienna with his eyes full of happy tears.

"It is," Sienna said as she approached Bob's bedside.

They hugged, and Bob sobbed a little. The burden and guilt he felt must've been more than Rita imagined.

"I can't believe I've been blessed to meet you, my daughter. Am I dreaming?" He asked, looking over at Rita, who was also in tears.

The emotions were so much. The three of them embraced and cried in sheer happiness. It was an amazing experience for them. They were a family. Rita and Bob had imagined what this moment would be like endless times, but this feeling was more than anything they could've ever imagined.

"How did you know I was your daughter?" Sienna asked as she took a seat on Bob's hospital bed.

"It was just instinct. " You got your good looks from me," Bob said with a wink.

"As you can see, Robert is very modest," Rita said with a laugh.

"I'm so happy to be here with you guys," Sienna said as she held Bob's hand.

The day shift nurse came to check on Bob. Sienna and Rita spoke with the nurse and were happy to hear that Bob was getting discharged tomorrow. They were ecstatic to hear Bob would be home in time for Christmas. The Christmas party wouldn't have been complete without him.

* * *

AFTER SPENDING the day with Bob in the hospital, Rita and Sienna returned home. Rita showed Sienna many photos of her and Bob during their teen years to more recent ones. She showed her pictures of her cousins and Mary Elle's family. Sienna mentioned how amazed she was at how much she looked like Bob. You could even pick up his sense of humor and spirit in the photographs.

As Rita showed Sienna around the house, she showed her some of Bob's baseball collection cards. Rita then showed Sienna her backyard, which was her pride and joy. She had worked hard to make it an oasis for her and Bob to relax and host barbecue parties. She was missing her plants, but they would get to work once winter was over.

"I know you might think this is crazy, but if you talk to your plants, they listen and will flourish if you speak loving words to them."

"I've always loved flowers and plants, but they just don't last for me. I guess I didn't get your green thumb."

"Maybe you are over-watering them or not giving them enough sunlight. Don't worry; I'll teach you everything I know when the time comes."

"Thank you. I'm already learning. Now I know I need to speak to them."

"Also, when you clean their leaves, it's as if you caress them. Try it next time."

"Rita, I love this time I'm spending with you. When I showed up here, I was so nervous. I didn't know how you would react or if you would want me in your life," Sienna said, and a single tear rolled down her face.

"Oh, honey," Rita said and pulled her into a deep embrace.

Once they were back inside the house, Rita shared about her trip to France with Mary Elle and how they had known each other for decades. Sienna commented that she felt as if she knew Mary Elle and her family. The friendship and connection between Rita and Mary Elle was beautiful and tangible.

"Will you stay the night?" Rita asked Sienna, as it was past midnight already. Time had flown by.

"It's pretty late, and I don't like driving at night in the mountains. There are lots of blind turns on the mountain." Sienna said.

"You are welcome to stay. The guest room is ready," Rita said as she guided her to the guest room and showed her the bathroom.

"So, you adopted your sister's kids when she lost custody?" Sienna asked as she sat on the guest bed.

"Yes, I did. I didn't want them to be alone in this world. Bob and I were already adults and had a house, and his business was doing well. If we could have kept you and given you a stable place, we would have kept you without a doubt. But we were just teens and didn't have any parental support or resources," Rita said, hoping to explain their decision.

"Yes, I understand. I know you couldn't look for me. I know you tried."

"I'm just happy I got to meet you. I know it happened in God's perfect timing," Rita said before pulling Sienna into another hug. She had to make up for all the years they had missed.

"I would love for you to meet your cousins," Rita said, hoping that Sienna would agree.

"That's a great idea. I would love that, too," Sienna said, giving away a small yawn.

"Get some rest. Tomorrow we are going to visit Bob," Rita said. She didn't know how Bob would take this surprise but was sure he would be pleased.

* * *

MARY ELLE WAS in the office reviewing vendor invoices and matching them to their corresponding events when Thomas came in. He placed a warm cup of tea on her coaster.

Mary Elle sniffed the air. "Mmm, mango green tea. My favorite. Thank you," she said as she took a sip.

"Only the very best, for my lady," Thomas said as he kissed the top of her head.

Mary Elle was sure she had won the lottery when she met Thomas. She had never known love the way he loved her. Sure, she had some fond memories of her ex-husband, but things with Thomas were utterly different.

Thomas took the seat in front of Mary Elle's desk, and she could tell something was on his mind.

"What's wrong?"

"Nothing. I'm just wondering how you're doing. Yesterday was a big day for you and quite eventful."

"It was stressful with the three events, but they all went off without a hitch. However, I think I won't be planning so many events on the same day in the future."

"Right, but what about Rita and Sienna? How do you feel about that?"

Mary Elle was still shocked to learn about Rita's daughter and the adoption.

"I'm alright, just as surprised as the rest of us. None of us had any idea what Rita and Bob went through. I hope Sienna brings Rita and Bob lots of joy."

"It must have been the best solution to their situation at the time, especially if their families weren't supportive. They were just kids at the time."

"I can't imagine how hard it must have been for them," Mary Elle said.

She knew Sienna was still in town, and she was letting Rita have some alone time with her, so she hadn't been able to talk to her much about it.

"The Sheriff came by the office today," Thomas said.

"Why?" Mary Elle asked, looking up from her work.

"I'm sure you've heard about the body they found?"

"Yes, I can't believe that happened here in Willow Heights."

"They identified the body," Thomas said.

Mary Elle's heart dropped. That probably meant it was someone from their small town.

"Who is it?" she asked softly.

"It's a young girl that lived in Winding Creek," Thomas said with a haunted look.

"Oh no," Mary Elle said, and she instantly felt sadness for the girl and her family.

It must be tough for them, and Mary Elle couldn't even imagine how terrified the girl must have been when this happened to her.

"I know," Thomas said, standing behind her with his hands on her shoulders.

"I pray God fills her family with peace during this difficult time," Mary Elle said, looking at Thomas.

"May God comfort them," Thomas said before placing a kiss on the top of Mary Elle's head.

"I want to send her family some flowers and a casserole."

Thomas nodded and said, "Let's get you home."

"I want to visit Melanie's house for a quick visit."

"That's a great idea. Cade wanted me to pass by; let me grab my keys."

"I'll shut down the computer and grab my purse."

* * *

TO THEIR SURPRISE, Rita was also visiting Melanie. Mary Elle hugged Rita as soon as she saw her.

"How are you, my dear?"

"Mary Elle, I worried you might be mad at me," Rita said

"Rita, I could never be mad at you. I am so happy for you. I can't imagine how you must feel after finally reconnecting with your daughter after all these years."

"It's been so great. Sienna spent the night, and we talked about everything, and I showed her old photos of us, and it was just a great night."

"That's beautiful, Rita. I'm so happy for you. I can't believe you had a baby, and I did not know! You sneaky girl," Mary Elle said, shaking her finger at her and laughing.

"I'm sorry, Mary Elle. I was just so ashamed about everything. Our parents were not supportive at all. I'm just happy Bob stayed with me even after all the drama and having to give up our baby. I've lived with this secret, and it was eating me up. It kept me from having another baby."

"I know you had no other choice. I understand, and I'm not upset. Rita, I love you so much!"

"As do I, Mary Elle." The best friends held each other and cried tears of joy.

"Hi, mom," Melanie said softly as she came out of Ryders' nursery, and Mary Elle embraced her.

"Hi Thomas," Cade said, looking out of place. There was so much emotion going on with the ladies.

"Hey, Cade, what's going on with the furnace?"

"I need to replace it; we've been using the chimney to stay warm. I'm afraid it's not warm enough for the baby, and we are soon going into full winter weather."

"Let's take a look," Thomas said as he followed Cade into the basement.

Rita, Melanie, and Mary Elle settled down, and Melanie brought them some tea, cream, sugar, and cookies. The chimney was on, and the wood was crackling in the fire.

"Sienna is so much like Bob; it's like having a mini-Bob," Rita said with a bittersweet tone. She wished she could've spent more time with Sienna, but Sienna had to return to work.

"I can't even imagine how happy Uncle Bob must have been to see her," Melanie said as she served the tea.

"Is she staying with you?" Mary Elle asked, already imagining a small get-together to welcome Sienna into the family.

"No, she had to go back. She said she would call me to make plans for the holidays."

"Your holidays will be filled with so much love, and joy, Rita," Mary Elle said as she touched Rita's hand.

"I hope her family doesn't mind," Rita said with a small sigh.

"These holidays will be amazing for all of us. We have new family members. Everything has happened in its perfect timing." Melanie said, smiling while looking at Ryder's baby photos on top of the chimney shelf.

"It's been a rough year for Bob and me, but I'm grateful Sienna found us. As for Alexander, Amanda, and Andrew, I cannot complain. I have everything I need."

"We are all grateful to have you and your beautiful family," Mary Elle said as she hugged Rita.

"So, how's our little man doing? Is he keeping you up late?" Rita asked Melanie, who was still adjusting to her new role as a mother.

He was born a few weeks earlier than expected, but like Melanie said, "it was the perfect time." Melanie's pregnancy had been difficult initially because she suffered from terrible morning sickness and lost a lot of weight. Still, the rest of her pregnancy had been smooth sailing from that first trimester. Ryder's delivery only lasted about 17 hours. He was a healthy baby, and Melanie had him naturally.

"Ryder is great, growing. He's always hungry, and he's keeping me busy at night. He sleeps during the day; that's when I catch up on sleep and cleaning and things around the house," Melanie said, yawning.

She missed sleeping in, but she wouldn't trade sleep for Ryder. He was everything to her. She had never felt such a love for someone as she did for Ryder. He was beautiful. She loved to stare at him while he was asleep. He smiled a lot when he was sleeping.

Ryder had a sweet personality; although he was still tiny, his character flourished. Melanie took several photographs of Ryder; she made a digital and print photo diary of him and how he changed as he grew.

"How are things with Cade?" Mary Elle asked.

"They've been great. He's so good with Ryder and comes by for a bit every day after work."

"He did an amazing job with the home repairs and

Ryder's nursery. It's beautiful," Rita mentioned while gazing over the living room; the house had an open floor plan allowing a full view from the entry to the kitchen to the living room area.

Thomas and Cade came upstairs from the basement and had made plans to put in a new furnace tomorrow evening. It was getting late; Mary Elle and Thomas said their goodbyes and left Melanie's house.

"I better get going as well," Rita said.

"Thank you for visiting Rita. We have to make plans to go plant shopping. We can do the landscaping ourselves. I told Cade we should leave an area in the backyard for my little gardening section."

"I would love that! I have some ideas about plants that will look beautiful all year round. We can also make a small greenhouse for the winter months if you'd like. Let me know if you have time this weekend. If not, we can always start after the holidays."

"I will let you know if Tiffany will be in town this weekend, and maybe she can babysit Ryder for me."

"Bye, darling."

They hugged goodbye, and Rita was on her way back home.

CHAPTER 8

$\mathcal{I}$t was finally the day of the long-awaited annual Christmas party. However, as always, things never go according to plan. The cold weather had caused a pipe to burst in Mary Elle's home. Although the weather was said to be clear today, they were getting heavy snow.

"I don't know how I feel about driving in this snow," Rita said as she looked out the window.

She was supposed to pick Bob up from the hospital, but she didn't have experience driving in the mountains, let alone with the snow they were getting. She didn't even know if her tires could handle driving in this weather.

"I can pick up Bob. We'll be back in time for the party," Thomas said.

He had come over as soon as he heard Mary Elle's pipe burst. He turned off the main water valve and helped clean it up.

"Would you do that?" Rita asked.

"Of course, don't worry about it."

Mary Elle came back with a small weekender bag she had packed.

"Thank you for letting me stay with you, Rita. I'll grab my toothbrush, and we can go to your house," Mary Elle said.

Thomas followed close behind her.

"Why don't you stay at my house?" Thomas asked her once they were alone.

Mary Elle said nothing at first. It hadn't even crossed her mind to stay with him.

"I just thought Rita might need me," she said.

Thomas nodded, but Mary Elle could tell he wasn't happy with her response.

"I'm sorry, Thomas. I can stay with you if you'd like," she said.

"No, it's okay, Mary Elle. I don't want to keep pressuring you into things you don't want."

"It's not that."

"It's okay, honey. You don't need to explain," Thomas said with a sad smile. He placed a quick kiss on her cheek and left.

Mary Elle stayed in place, unsure of what had just happened. Why were things with Thomas suddenly so complicated? They were so happy before. The engagement should've brought them closer together. Instead, she felt like things were slowly falling apart.

* * *

RITA NOTICED Sienna's car parked outside her house once they got back. She quickly shut off the engine and jumped out of her car.

Sienna stepped out of her car at the same time Rita did.

"Sienna, I can't believe you're here!" she said, pulling her into a hug.

"Hi Rita, sorry to show up unannounced," Sienna said once they pulled apart.

"Is everything ok?" Rita asked as she looked her over.

"Yes, I just wanted to revisit you. I came as soon as I got out of work. Is Bob home yet?"

"Not yet, but he should be here soon. I'm so happy you're here."

"Hi, Mary Elle," Sienna said when Mary Elle joined them.

"Welcome back to Willow Heights, Sienna; you're just in time for our annual Christmas party!"

Rita opened the front door, turned on the lights, and hung her purse and keys. Penny greeted her and demanded her food.

Sienna walked in after Rita and Penny went over to sniff her before going back to begging for her dinner.

Mary Elle excused herself to give them time to catch up.

"Hi Penny, remember me?" Sienna asked as she crouched down and spoiled Penny with belly rubs.

Penny ate her food and quickly went to sleep in her little corner. Penny wasn't an excellent guard dog, but Rita loved and spoiled her.

Penny now had a room and closet with cute little outfits, raincoats, shoes, hats, Halloween costumes, and everything you could imagine a spoiled little dog could have. Not to mention her bed and toys and harness collection. They had converted the linen closet into her little room. Bob had even installed a small puppy door for her to enter her room as she pleased. Rita had contemplated getting a puppy to keep Penny company, but she didn't know if Penny would be happy with having to share all the attention and her room with someone else.

Noticing that Penny was already fast asleep, Rita said, "Sorry, she's too tired to be social."

"It's ok; I grew up with dogs and cats. We even had a little pig named Piglet."

"That's so funny. We wanted to have a little pig too, but

Bob said no. The kids wanted a cat, but Bob was allergic. We've had Penny for about eight years. She is our baby."

"I can see she knows she's the queen of the house,"

"How was work?" Rita asked now that they were sitting in the living room.

"Work was hectic. Being a nurse is overwhelming sometimes. I haven't had time to visit my family. I worked 12-hour shifts and lived closer to the hospital; their house is about 25 minutes away."

"I'm so proud of you. The nurses that took care of Bob were amazing. To be a nurse, I know you have to be a caring person. It has to be a passion for helping others."

"Yes, it's my passion. I love seeing my patients thrive and go home better than when they arrived at the hospital. I came to visit you to ask for advice. I've been thinking of becoming a traveling nurse. Which is kind of scary but exciting at the same time."

"What is a traveling nurse?"

"Well, I'll travel around the country for different assignments. Some contracts or assignments only last a few months before moving to the next state."

"That sounds like fun and adventurous. But what's keeping you from making that change in your career?"

"Well, not much. It's just that I finally found you, and I would have to move after the holidays if I moved forward with this change. Also, I would have to give up my apartment and put some things in storage. I'll take my essentials, but I can sell or put the rest in storage."

"Don't worry about me. We can arrange a time to visit each other. I've always wanted to travel within the USA as well. This will give me an excuse to either drive or fly. I won't mind at all. About your things, we can have a garage sale. I can also keep some of your things in my spare room," Rita said with a small laugh.

"I can work with that. I didn't want you to think that meeting you after all these years wasn't meaningful to me because it was. Rita, I'm so happy to have found you."

"I know. I'm thrilled with having you here and you expressing your concern. That means so much to me. It's like I'm part of you and your life, which was something I never thought would be possible. I'm so proud of you and grateful that your parents raised you to be such a great person."

Rita offered her some food, realizing that Sienna might be hungry from her long drive.

"Would you like a little snack before the party? I have some leftover pasta I can heat."

"Sure, I can have some pasta with you."

"Excellent," Rita said as she heated their food.

Rita got some garlic bread rolls and heated them as well. She got wine glasses and her favorite Moscato wine out for them to enjoy.

"This pasta is amazing; did you make it?"

"Yes, I did. It's an old family recipe."

"You're Italian?"

Rita looked at her, smiling. "Did I forget to go over our heritage? Well, I'm half Italian and Honduran. I know a strange mix. Your grandfather, Jose, is Honduran. He came to the USA when he was very young. He was a shoemaker and had a small shoe store. My mother's family descends from Italy and has been here for some time. She was a server in her father's Italian restaurant back in Atlanta. My parents met when he went for dinner at her restaurant. He was actually on a date with another girl. They always said it was love at first sight, and here we are. Your father's family is from Ireland. They came here back in the late 1880s. Your father and I met in high school when his family moved from Boston to Atlanta. It was love at first sight, but I was too shy to talk to him. Mary Elle introduced us. She's never really been shy."

"Wow, that's amazing. I didn't know I was such an interesting blend."

"You're a beautiful mixture of all that's great in the world. Bob and I loved learning about our cultures. We embraced some things. My father taught me how to make tortillas and Honduran pastries. When I was small, my father took me to visit family in Honduras, and it was so beautiful. Your father's family is known for their fish and chips recipe. They make a special batter for the fish. They loved making that whenever we visited. Your cousins on Bob's side know how to river dance. It's wonderful. Bob and I haven't visited Italy, but it is on our bucket list." Rita said.

"Maybe we can visit Italy together one day," Sienna said.

"I would love that. I know Bob's family in Boston would also love to meet you. His parents passed away a couple of years ago. My father is the only one left for me. Your grandmother, Maria, passed away a few years ago. We should plan to take you to meet my father soon. It would delight him to meet you and see what a beautiful and amazing young lady you are."

"I can't wait to meet all my family members."

The two of them enjoyed each other's company and lunch. They had so much to share and so many questions to ask each other. It was like reuniting with your best friend after losing contact with them.

Rita marveled at Sienna's resemblance to Bob. Even some facial gestures Sienna made were precisely what Bob would do. It was uncanny.

* * *

THE GANG MET at Willow Acres for some final finishing touches. Christmas music filled the room, and everyone was in the holiday spirit.

"It's not Christmas without a mistletoe," Patty said as she and Lisa hung one at the barn entrance.

"I know who you might want to meet under the mistletoe," Tiffany said as she bumped shoulders with her aunt, making the Christmas bells on DeeAnn's sweater jingle.

The attire for today was the silliest Christmas sweater you could find, which was Mrs. Waskosky's doing.

Patty and Lisa let out a dramatic, "Ooooh."

"Tiffany, you're too much!" DeeAnn said, giggling.

Right on queue, Paul appeared holding a bottle of wine and a box of gingerbread cookies.

He wore a buffalo plaid Christmas sweater with a reindeer sporting a glowing red nose.

"Hello, ladies," he said as he gave the wine bottle and cookies to DeeAnn.

"Paul, welcome! I'd like to introduce you to Patty and Lisa. Patty takes care of the garden here in Willow Acres and makes the most gorgeous floral arraignments, and Lisa runs the gift shop and bakery here. Ladies, this is Paul from the Christmas tree farm."

"Pleased to meet you, ladies. Patty, you seem familiar. Do I know you from somewhere?"

"Yes, my mother worked at the tree farm for many years."

"I knew you looked familiar. I hope to catch up with your mother tonight," Paul said before turning to Tiffany. "Thank you for inviting me. I am thrilled to be here."

"Of course! Come in and get ready to have a great time," she said as she ushered him inside.

"Hi there, Mrs. Waskosky. Ready to get started?" Tiffany asked her.

Mrs. Waskosky had been working very hard on her Christmas game setup.

"I hope you're up to date with your Christmas movie trivia because the prize is great!"

"I love Christmas movies. What's the prize?" Tiffany asked.

Mrs. Waskosky tsked, "I'm not spoiling the surprise. Just know it's a good one."

Everyone was at the Christmas party, except for Thomas and Bob. Rita called home several times to see if Bob had made it there and changed to come to the party, but no one answered.

"Mary Elle, have you heard from Thomas? It's getting late, and they aren't here yet."

"No, I haven't heard from him. I'll try his cellphone."

Mary Elle called Thomas' cellphone, but he must be in a low reception area since it went straight to voicemail.

"I can't reach him; he must not have good reception. Did you call the hospital to see if they had discharged Bob? Maybe there's been a delay?"

"Good idea; I'll call the hospital."

A few minutes later, Rita came over to Mary Elle.

"He was discharged about two hours ago, and the Nurse saw Thomas with him. Where could they be now?'

"I'm not sure, Rita," Mary Elle said, looking outside and realizing the snow was coming down heavily and the roads must be very icy. "They're probably just taking it slow to be safe."

"Maybe we should drive to the hospital and see if they are stuck in the snow or something?" Rita suggested.

"Well, we could ask David or Cade to drive us there. I'm like you and have no experience driving in this amount of snow and on these dark curvy roads," Mary Elle said as she noticed a police car drive into Willow Acre's parking lot.

"Mary Elle, what's wrong?" Rita asked as she saw the look on Mary Elle's face change to a dreadful stare.

"Come, Rita, let's go see why those police officers are here," Mary Elle said as she grabbed Rita by her arm.

"Evening, ladies," Officer Sterling said.

"Good evening, officer," Mary Elle said, "Is everything alright?"

"Yes, we just came to inform you that Thomas and Robert were in a car accident outside Winding Creek. It happened near the hospital, and they were just taken to get checked to make sure everything is alright," Officer Sterling said calmly.

"Are they ok?" Rita asked, holding back tears.

"They got hit by a drunk driver, who is now in custody. Thomas' truck was wrecked pretty bad, but they are ok. They were transported to the hospital and are getting checked, but they were conscious and asked that I come to notify you since reception on that side of the mountain isn't available right now."

"Thank you, Officer Sterling. We'll drive up to the hospital to get them."

"Drive safely, ladies; there's a lot of snow and reckless drivers out tonight."

Mary Elle and Rita went back inside the barn to tell everyone what happened with Thomas and Bob. Cade and David offered to take them to the hospital before Mary Elle could ask.

During the drive, Mary Elle couldn't stop imagining the worse. She and Rita were a mess. What would they have done if the accident had been fatal? Life was so short and fragile.

David dropped them off in front of the hospital and went to find a parking spot.

"Rita, Sienna, boy, am I happy to see you!" Bob said as he saw them walking into his emergency hospital room.

"Bob, what happened?"

"A drunk driver drove us off the road. We are ok, thank God."

"What did the doctors say about your heart? Can you come home tonight?"

"Yes, we are both discharged. We are not hurt."

"Let's get you home," Rita said as she and Sienna got Bob and his belongings.

Meanwhile, Mary Elle and Thomas were talking in his hospital room. As soon as she saw him, she crashed into his arms and started crying.

"Hey, it's okay. I'm okay," Thomas said as he held her close.

"I don't know what I would've done if something happened to you," Mary Elle said as she took a step back to look into his eyes.

"Don't think like that. It was just a small scare."

"The officer said your car is wrecked."

"Well, yes. But I'm okay." Thomas said, holding his arms out.

Mary Elle looked him over and saw that he seemed fine, apart from a few scratches on his face.

"How are you?" David asked as he appeared next to Mary Elle.

"Never been better," Thomas said with a wink.

"Are you ready to go?" David asked as he looked him over.

"Yeah. Let's go to the Christmas Party before they eat all the pecan pie. I'm starving," Thomas said with a small laugh.

"All aboard?" Cade asked as everyone got in his car.

"Yes, sir," Sienna said, smiling.

"Let's get back to partying," Thomas said as he wrapped his arm around Mary Elle.

"You got it, boss," Cade replied while patting him on the arm.

"Bob, Rita, are you guys staying for the party?"

"Oh, I don't know. How are you feeling, Bob?"

"I'm ok. We can stop by the party and have some eggnog," Bob replied.

"Sounds like a plan," Rita said.

"So, you're going to need a new truck?" David asked Thomas.

"I guess if I can't fix old Martha."

"Old Martha?" David asked, laughing. "You named the old car Martha?"

"Sure did; she's one elegant, reliable lady."

* * *

"You guys! I've never been so happy to see you both." Melanie said as she saw Bob and Thomas walk into the barn.

"Don't you two ever scare us like that again!" Tiffany said with a playful scold on her face.

"We're fine. We just thought the night needed a little excitement," Thomas said with a wink.

"Can I hold that little boy?" Bob asked as he reached for Ryder, who was wide awake, enjoying the party. He loved all the twinkling lights.

"Here you go. Be careful; he just ate," Melanie said as she carefully handed Ryder to Bob.

DeeAnn walked over to them and gave Bob and Thomas a quick hug before saying, "We set up a photo area by the Christmas tree for everyone to take Polaroid pictures with their loved ones. We have some props there too."

She was walking away when she turned back around and said, "I'm sorry. Where are my manners? This is Paul. He is the owner of the tree farm where we got these amazing Christmas trees. Paul, this is everyone. Too many people to introduce," she said with a laugh.

"Nice to meet you," Mary Elle said.

"Nice to meet you all. This party is great. Thanks for having me."

"Please enjoy the party," Mary Elle said as David approached her to tell her the food was ready. And if she could give a speech because Thomas wasn't up for it.

"Good evening, everyone. It's such a blessing to see you all here. We wanted to honor all our friends and family this Christmas and share this special day. Earlier this evening, we had a scare with Bob and Thomas, but God was faithful and protected them and kept them safe in his hands. God has blessed us with health and love. We would like for you all to enjoy this feast and have fun! Merry Christmas!" Mary Elle walked over to their table and sat next to Thomas. His hand found hers, and he gave her a gentle squeeze. She looked over at him, and when their eyes met, she felt her heart warm.

CHAPTER 9

Once everyone finished their meals, David returned to his DJ booth to get the party going again. Soon everyone was dancing and having a great time.

"May I have this dance?" Cade asked Melanie.

"Of course," Melanie said as she moved a sleeping Ryder in his stroller towards Rita, sitting with Bob and Sienna.

"Thanks, Rita," Melanie said, squeezing her shoulder.

"You look beautiful as always, Melanie," Cade said as he took her hand.

"Thank you. You always know just what to say," Melanie said and was glad it was dark enough that he couldn't see she was blushing.

Cade always made her feel like a million bucks. How did she get so lucky to have found someone who loved her and constantly reminded her of how special she was?

"Michael!" Melanie said as she noticed her brother walk into the barn with an older woman.

"I finally made it. Our flight was delayed, and I called mom, but she didn't answer."

"It's been a crazy night. I'm so glad you could make it," she said, hugging her brother.

"I want you to meet Samantha. She's my fiancée," Michael said, putting his arm around Samantha.

They finished their introductions, and Melanie returned to the dance floor where Cade was waiting for her. Sienna and Jasper were dancing close by, and she shared a smile with her. Melanie looked over at Bob and Rita as they held Ryder, and she felt a slight ache in her heart. She couldn't fathom how difficult it must have been for them to have given Sienna up.

* * *

MARY ELLE and Thomas were slow dancing, enjoying the night. The snow outside was still falling, but they were all warm and cozy inside the barn. She was happy, and her heart was whole. She couldn't imagine being anywhere else but here.

"What are you thinking?" Thomas asked.

"That I'm exactly where I am meant to be," Mary Elle said, and she meant it with all her heart.

"And where is that?" Thomas asked with a raised brow.

"In Willow Heights, in your arms, surrounded by everyone we love."

She felt a light tap on her shoulder and slowly turned to find Michael standing there.

"Michael!" she said as she quickly pulled him into a hug.

"Hi, mom, I've missed you," Michael said as they hugged.

"I've missed you too, sweetheart," Mary Elle said, placing a hand on his cheek.

Thomas greeted Michael and Michael introduced them to Samantha.

"It's good to see you, Thomas. I want you guys to meet my beautiful fiancée, Samantha."

Mary Elle had noticed the woman standing next to Michael, but she would've never guessed that she was his fiancée. She looked much older than him.

"Welcome to Willow Heights," Thomas said to her.

Mary Elle knew she had to say something, but the only thing that came out was, "Welcome. Enjoy the party!"

She hoped she had not appeared rude. She was just surprised. Mary Elle would accept her kids' love interests as long as they loved and respected her kids. Samantha must be exceptional to have captured her son's heart and attention. She knew her boy was not that easy to tame.

* * *

"Okay, now that you've all eaten and danced your hearts out, it's time for the party!" Mrs. Waskosky said from the front of the barn on a makeshift stage David created that morning. She was standing next to David with a mic in hand.

Everyone cheered in excitement. Tiffany had been waiting for this all night. Party games were her favorite part of the night.

"In this cup, I have everyone's names," Mrs. Waskosky said, holding a red solo cup and shaking it. "I will pull out names at random to decide teams."

Melanie squeezed Tiffany's hand and said, "I hope we're on the same team!"

Mrs. Waskosky turned to David and said, "Go have a seat. No more DJing; you got to play."

David didn't want to play, but he obediently went to take a seat.

Mrs. Waskosky called out names, and soon six different teams were formed.

The first game was a Christmas Bingo, of course. They also played put the nose on the reindeer, which Dean won. They played the antler toss game, where the team leader had to wear a reindeer head, the team had to throw rings and the team that could catch the most rings won. When his team won, Cade broke into a moonwalk dance ala Michael Jackson. In between games, they took breaks to decorate gingerbread houses. Everyone was having a great time and buzzing with excitement. Mrs. Waskosky had gone above and beyond.

After many games, the last two teams with the most points faced off. Tiffany and Sienna were the team leaders. The previous game was Christmas Family Feud.

"Are you ready to go down?" Tiffany asked Sienna as their teams cheered for them.

Mrs. Waskosky laughed, "Ok, for the last question: What is the main villain's name in The Nightmare Before Christmas?"

The room went quiet, and the last two teams stood huddled together.

"I know this. It's on the tip of my tongue," Patty said.

"Think, Patty, think!" Lisa said.

"That's the only Christmas movie I've never watched," Tiffany said, feeling defeated.

The other team rang their bell, and David stood next to Mrs. Waskosky.

"The main villain's name in The Nightmare Before Christmas is Oogie Boogie," he said into the mic with a proud smile.

"That is correct!" Mrs. Waskosky said, giving David a high five.

"Noooo," Tiffany's team cried out.

"Since you're the winning team, you each win a prize at Winding Creeks spa. You will have a massage, champagne, and dinner for you and a guest!" Mrs. Waskosky said, and the winning team cheered as they jumped up and down in excitement.

"This has been the best Christmas Party we have had in a very long time," Tiffany said.

"It was a success, and it should be a new tradition to host this kind of party for Christmases to come," David said, waving the envelope with the gift cards to Winding Creek.

He loved the opportunity to rub it in Tiffany's and her team's faces.

"My team will win next year. Enjoy your gloating while you can!" Tiffany said as she poked out her tongue at David.

"Kids these days," Melanie said with a smile as she witnessed their interaction.

"Mrs. Waskosky, everyone had an amazing time with all the games and the excitement. Thank you for helping us entertain the guests and the wonderful prizes for the winning team," Mary Elle said as she placed an arm around Mrs. Waskosky, who was so proud of how well everything turned out.

"You're most welcome, Mary Elle. I enjoyed it too. George is my brother, so I just had to bother him for a week until he agreed," Mrs. Waskosky laughed.

"Elle, we're leaving soon; Bob's tired," Rita said as she appeared next to them.

"It's ok, don't worry. Do you want Thomas to drive you home?" Mary Elle said as she turned to face her.

"That would be great. Thank you."

"No worries. I'll let him know. Did Sienna enjoy the party?" Mary Elle said as she and Rita went in search of Thomas.

"She did. She's excited about meeting the kids."

The three were supposed to be here today, but life had other plans. Alexander and Caroline went to South Carolina to surprise her family with the baby news. Andrew and Amanda stayed in Atlanta. Amanda wanted to spend Christmas with friends, and Andrew had a work event. Rita hadn't told them about Sienna because that was too personal and complicated to discuss over the phone.

"Please let me know if you need any help with anything," Mary Elle said as she hugged Rita goodbye.

"No worries. I'll make Andrew's favorite dish, Alex's favorite dessert, and Mandy's favorite appetizer. You know, so they all feel loved and special."

"I know. Did you meet Samantha?" Mary Elle asked Rita in a hushed voice.

She didn't want anyone to overhear and think they gossiped about her.

"Yeah, she seems older than him, but I'm sure she's a very nice lady," Rita said, careful not to judge a book by its cover.

"You're right. If she's captured Michael's heart this much, she's a catch," Mary Elle said, sounding concerned.

"All you have to do is pray. God will show Michael if this is the right time and person to settle down with."

"You're always right. God will take care of it; he always does," Mary Elle said as she hugged Rita goodbye again and wished her a Merry Christmas.

This made their friendship so special. They both reminded each other to stay focused on what truly mattered and trust God. Despite challenging times, they had each other's support to rely on, and their faith never wavered.

* * *

As Rita and Bob were leaving the Christmas Party, he stopped abruptly as they were about to go through the barn doors.

87

"Rita, after all these years, you are still the only one that takes my breath away. How did I get so lucky with you?"

"Oh, Bob. You are the love of my life. I love you so much," Rita replied as she looked up, saw the mistletoe, and realized why Bob had stopped there to express his love for her. They shared a sweet, tender kiss representing their relationship and love for each other.

CHAPTER 10

Cade brought Melanie and Ryder home and helped her get settled in. It was past midnight, but she invited him in because they hadn't exchanged gifts yet.

"Here's a little gift from Ryder and me," Melanie said as she handed Cade a small red, white and green plaid patterned gift box.

They were now seated in her living room, and Ryder was in the bassinet Melanie kept in the living room for him.

"What is it?" Cade asked as he shook the small box for clues.

"Open it!" Melanie said, hoping Cade would like the small gift inside.

She'd seen it at an outdoor shop outside of town, and it had instantly made her think of him.

"I love it. Thank you." Cade said as he hugged her and then studied the gift.

It was a matte black pocket utility knife with a red blade and his name engraved on it. Cade collected them and showed Melanie his small collection when she first visited his cabin.

"You're welcome. I'm so happy you love it!" Melanie said, beaming with pride.

"Since we are exchanging gifts, this one is for my boy, Ryder," Cade said as he handed her a big box wrapped in blue and silver snowflakes wrapping paper.

"Ryder, your first Christmas gift on your first Christmas!" Melanie exclaimed as she helped Ryder open his gift. At first glance, she noticed the box was filled with different wooden toys and a sensory bin full of fun goodies.

"This is such a thoughtful gift. Thank you, Cade."

"Look through it; it has many more goodies," Cade said, smiling and helping Melanie pull out different teething toys, a small giraffe plush toy, a few onesies, socks, and books.

"Cade, you got him so many things. I love it all, and I'm sure he does, too. Don't you, Ryder?" Melanie said as she gently kissed his forehead.

"And this one is for you, Melanie," Cade said as he handed her a small box.

"It's beautiful, thank you, Cade," Melanie said as she leaned in to kiss him.

She studied the locket and was touched by his sweet gift. It was a gold heart with tiny stars and little diamonds in the center of the stars.

"Here, let me help you put it on," Cade said as he lifted Melanie's long, dark brown hair to close the clasp for her.

"I love it," Melanie said, placing her hand over it. "I can't wait to show my mom and Tiffany."

"You can open the locket," Cade said as he helped her open it to find a special surprise he had done for Melanie.

"Oh my, it has Ryder's photo!"

"I left the other side empty, so you can put any photo you like."

"Thank you. This is the best gift," she said as tears formed in her eyes.

Melanie couldn't get over how thoughtful and caring Cade was with her and little Ryder. He loved them both so much. She never thought she would get to experience a love so pure and true. Melanie had never known love like the love that Cade showed her every day.

* * *

It had been a few days since Christmas, and Rita loved the time she spent with Sienna. She wasn't supposed to be back at work until the new year and had stayed with Rita and Bob. The rest of the kids would come over for dinner today, and Rita couldn't wait for them to meet Sienna. Their family was complete now. She didn't have to wonder what had happened to the baby. She had to give up so long ago. She was here now, and they were a family again.

The food was ready, and they set the table up. Rita was doing some last-minute dusting because she couldn't sit still.

"Honey, you're making me dizzy. Please have a seat," Bob said as he patted the spot on the sofa next to him.

"I can't. There's still much to do, and our house is messy."

"A mess? You've been cleaning nonstop for days. I feel like I'm in a fancy museum instead of my home. I'm scared even to touch anything."

Rita giggled and took the seat next to Bob on the sofa.

"Oh, Robert, I'm just so excited. Our family is complete!" Rita said as she rested her head on his.

"I know. We've always wanted this," Bob said as he rested his head on Rita's.

They sat there enjoying the moment. Their hearts had yearned for this for so long. God's faithfulness was proving itself once again in their lives.

Sienna walked in and hung up her coat. "it's freezing out there!" she shook herself off.

"How was your lunch?" Rita asked as she sat up.

Sienna had gone out for lunch with Melanie and Tiffany.

"It was nice. I like the girls. Honestly, I have no complaints about this town or the people."

"It makes me very happy to hear that."

"Rita, Bob, I want to say I'm so grateful to be here. It's been a blessing and a prayer that God answered," Sienna said.

"Sienna, I hope you know that we have loved you ever since we both knew we conceived you. Our love for you led us to give you a better opportunity in life. As teen parents, without the support of our own families, we couldn't guarantee you a future. We didn't know if we would drift apart during and after the pregnancy. We didn't know what the future held for us, but we never stopped loving you. You were always in our prayers and thoughts, and we felt guilty all these years. We tried looking for you, but the adoption agency couldn't provide us any information on you or your adoptive parents," Rita said as she held Sienna's hand, and Bob hugged them. It was a tender and emotional moment for them.

"I know. I'm trying to understand and put myself in your shoes. I felt like something was missing all my life, and now I realize it was you guys," Sienna said as she hugged them back.

"It's truly amazing how God brought us all back. He allowed me to have this extra time on Earth to meet you. He knew this was what I always dreamed of. Sienna, you are everything we both wanted you to be. We are so proud of who you have become because you allowed us into your life. I hope you can forgive us for giving you up as a baby," Bob said as he wiped the tears off his face.

"Of course I do. I love you guys."

"We love you too," Rita said as she kissed the top of Sienna's head.

A few minutes later, there was a knock on the door, and Rita felt her heart speed up.

"They're here!" she said as she looked at herself in the mirror before opening the door.

Alexander, Andrew, Amanda, and Caroline stood there waiting to be let in.

"Welcome, welcome," Rita said as she held the door open for them.

Caroline handed her a small gift, and they all said their hellos and exchanged hugs. Sienna stood quietly behind, watching them. Alexander was the first to notice her.

"Hello," he said.

"Hi," she replied shyly.

"We have a special announcement," Bob said as he stood in front of the fireplace, "come have a seat, kids."

Everyone took a seat on the living room sofa. Rita stood next to him, unable to hide the huge smile on her face.

"Sienna," Bob said as he gestured for her to join them.

"We would like you all to meet Sienna," Rita said as she looked at their faces.

"A long time ago, when Rita and I were in high school, we had a baby," Bob said.

Amanda brought her hand to her face and let out a small gasp. The boys sat expressionlessly, and Caroline's eyes were as wide as saucers.

"Our parents made us give her up for adoption, and after many years of wondering what might have happened to her, she showed up on our doorstep now a full-grown adult," Rita said with tears.

Amanda jumped off her seat and wrapped Rita and Bob in a hug before introducing herself to Sienna. Caroline followed close behind.

"So, she's our cousin?" Andrew asked.

"Yes," Bob answered.

"Why didn't you ever tell us?" Alexander asked with anger in his voice.

"We were ashamed. No one ever knew. Our parents made us promise that we wouldn't tell anyone."

"I can't believe this," Alexander said and stormed out of the house.

Caroline ran after him.

Rita looked over at Bob, but he was as confused as her about his reaction.

"I'm sorry," Sienna said as she approached Rita.

"It's okay; you did nothing wrong."

"It's just a shock. He'll be okay," Andrew said, reassuring her. He took a seat next to Rita and hugged her.

"We should go talk to him," Rita told Bob.

Bob nodded, and together they made their way outside.

Caroline and Alexander were talking outside his car. When she saw them approaching, Caroline's eyes were filled with concern.

"Can we talk?" Bob asked as they approached.

Alexander didn't say anything. He shrugged and wiped away the angry tears coming down his face.

"I'll give you guys some privacy," Caroline said as she wrapped her cardigan closer around herself.

"Thank you," Rita said as Caroline walked by her on her way back inside the house.

"What's going on, son?" Bob asked as he sat next to Alexander on the hood of his truck.

"I don't know," Alexander said.

"I'm sorry that we never told you guys about her. It wasn't our intention to hurt you," Rita said as she gently touched his cheek.

"Did you only take us in out of guilt? Because you felt like you had to because you had already given a child up?" Alexander said as he stared down at his feet.

Rita was entirely caught off guard. How could he feel this way? She and Bob had done everything they could to always make the kids feel loved and not make them feel like a burden. They had never regretted their decision. Taking the kids in was one of the best decisions they ever made.

"Of course not," Bob said, and he looked over at Rita, unsure of what else to say.

"We love you, Alex. We have always loved you. Bob and I would've taken you all in regardless of the situation. You are our family, and nothing or anyone will change that."

"How do you know she's even who she says she is? Some stranger shows up at your house, and you accept it? What if she's using you? Maybe she wants money."

Sienna had come outside with none of them noticing and let out a gasp before running back inside the house.

"Alexander, I will not let you speak ill of her in our home. I understand you're upset, but this is no way to act," Bob said as Rita followed Sienna inside the house to ensure she was okay.

"You can come inside and talk this out the way we raised you to, or you can leave."

Without saying a word, Alexander got in his car and drove off.

* * *

DeeAnn and Mary Elle showed up at Rita's house the next day to keep her company. Rita called them as soon as the kids left.

"Rita, I am so sorry. I know how much you were looking forward to the kids meeting Sienna," DeeAnn said as she placed a warm bowl of soup in front of her.

DeeAnn swore that her special homemade chicken noodle soup was the cure for everything. Feeling like a cold is coming on? Chicken noodle soup. Feeling blue? Chicken noodle soup, of course.

Rita blew her nose. Her nose and eyes were red from crying. She had never expected the night to go down like that.

"Alexander will come around. I'm sure it was just a shock to him," Mary Elle said with a sympathetic smile.

"I know. I think what hurts the most is that Alexander reacted that way. I expected it from Amanda, maybe. Not Alex, my sweet boy," Rita said as the tears came down again.

Alexander had always been the one that held the closest bond with Rita. They have shared a very special relationship since he was a young boy. He had witnessed most of his mother's struggles and had been affected the most by them. Because of that, Rita always dedicated the most time and attention to him.

"I hate seeing you like this," DeeAnn said with tears in her eyes.

DeeAnn could never see anyone cry because she would start crying as well.

"Okay, enough of this," Mary Elle said as she wiped a tear from her face, "We didn't come here to cry. We came to lift you up. So, you're going to eat your soup, and then we're going out. So, hurry up and get dressed."

They finished their food and drove to Winding Creek. There was a nail salon that served you champagne and gave you a complimentary facial while you got your nails done. Rita seemed in better spirits as they sat there getting their nails done.

"I haven't seen you, ladies, around before. Where are you visiting from?" The salon manager asked as she approached them. Her name tag said her name was Lorna.

"We all moved to Willow Heights recently," DeeAnn told her.

DeeAnn was the only one that hadn't started getting her facial done yet. Rita and Mary Elle were both reclined back and getting a steam facial to begin.

"How nice. I've heard that great things are happening in Willow Heights. A magazine article even said it's the next up-and-coming family vacation destination."

"That's right! Mary Elle and I visited here with our parents when we were kids."

"Mary Elle? Why does that name sound familiar?" Lorna asked, looking over to the esthetician.

"Isn't she the one dating Clarice's Thomas?" one of the manicurists said.

"Oh," Lorna said and walked away.

Once the ladies were done getting their nails done and shopping, they went to The Sneaky Cat Pub in Winding Creek.

"Wasn't that awkward?" DeeAnn said as she dipped her shrimp in cocktail sauce.

"I know! I was about to say something but decided against it," Rita said with a laugh as she recalled the moment.

"The best part was when she said 'Clarice's Thomas,' I had to hold back my laugh so hard," Mary Elle said.

"That was the icing on the cake," Rita said as she dumped her Zucchini fry into a small tub of ranch dressing.

"What do they put on these wings? They are so good!" Mary Elle said.

"A lot of grease and love," Lauren, their server, said as she returned to their table to refill their drinks.

"Love always makes everything taste better," DeeAnn said between bites.

"So, I hope you all don't have any plans for New Year," Mary Elle said.

"Are you planning on hosting another party so soon?" Rita asked her.

"Is this your way of postponing your wedding? You keep throwing parties, hoping we won't notice? Trust me; we're noticing," DeeAnn said as she bumped her shoulder.

Mary Elle rolled her eyes and said, "I want to hold a small get-together for New Year's at my house. Nothing fancy."

"You completely ignored my comment about your wedding."

"I didn't ignore it. Thomas and I will get married when the time is right, which isn't right now." Mary Elle said with a shrug.

Rita and DeeAnn exchanged a look but said nothing.

CHAPTER 11

"*M*ost people wait until after the new year," Melanie said, wiping the sweat off her forehead with a towel.

"Why wait when you can start now?" Tiffany said, a little too excited for Melanie's liking.

A new gym opened up in Willow Heights, and they were offering four months for the price of one to the first 20 people who signed up. Tiffany had seen the flyer while decorating the square for Christmas and had signed herself and Melanie up.

"We should start with the StairMaster," Tiffany said as she rushed over to the StairMaster area as if anyone was trying to race her to one. She quickly set it up for three miles.

This was going to be a long workout session, Melanie thought. She dragged her feet over to the StairMaster next to Tiffany's.

"So, I talked to Mandy," Tiffany said when Melanie joined her.

"What did she say?"

"Well, she and Andrew are happy for Rita and Bob, but Alexander didn't take the news very well."

"Poor Alex," Melanie said, trying to catch her breath while exercising and talking.

She knew this must've caught him by surprise, but she did not doubt that he would come around. Alexander was a sweetheart to his core, and he probably just needed a little time to wrap his head around it. Melanie and her siblings had always been close to Rita's kids growing up. Alexander and Andrew had always watched over her and Tiffany as their little sisters, too.

"How are things going with Cade?"

"They're great. He's great. I do not know how I got so lucky. Honestly, I wasn't even looking to meet anyone. I thought I would be single for a while after Everett."

"You know what they say; love comes when you least expect it."

"That's true. So, is there a special guy that caught your eye? Is that why you're dragging us to this torture chamber?"

"Torture chamber?" Tiffany repeated with a laugh.

"Don't avoid the question!" Melanie said as she struggled to keep up with the StairMaster.

"I'm not avoiding and no boys. I am focused on my career and just being healthy for myself."

"Uh-huh," Melanie said.

"It's the truth!" Tiffany said as she flawlessly kept up with the StairMaster.

"I didn't say anything," Melanie said, pretending to be shocked at the accusation.

"I love that Willow Heights is growing, and all these new businesses are opening up, but I miss how it was when we first moved here, and it felt like this was our little secret getaway."

"What do you mean? New businesses are opening, but it's

all locals. The big guys haven't tried to throw their hats in the race yet."

"It's just a matter of time," Tiffany said with a sigh.

"Did you like Samantha?" Melanie asked out of nowhere.

"Well, Michael is strange with the women he's dated, but I never pictured him with an older woman before."

"I don't know. She seems familiar to me, but I can't quite place her. She seemed nice and polite. Has mom mentioned anything to you about her?"

"Nope, nothing. I know mom invited Michael and Samantha for her New Year's dinner."

"Have you spoken with Dad recently?" Melanie asked as she got off the StairMaster to drink water and wipe the sweat from her brow.

"I last spoke with him during Christmas. He was on his way to Hawaii with Barbara," Tiffany said.

"Oh, that's nice. I got a text message and a snapshot of his face."

"He and Barb seem happy together. I'm also happy for mom and Thomas. I can see their love for each other."

"Me too, but strangely, mom isn't talking about or planning her wedding yet."

"They just got engaged, Mel. I don't think they need to rush into anything. Let mom enjoy the single life a little longer. She deserves it."

"I guess you're right."

"Are you in a rush to marry Cade?"

"I would love to marry Cade, and he recently commented on us getting married."

"No way! Did he?"

"Yep," Melanie said, unable to hide her smile.

"I'm so happy for you, Mel. I like Cade for you."

"Thanks. Are you thinking about moving to Willow Heights? I know things aren't going well at work. Mom would be over the moon if you moved here. I would love to have you close! I don't like you driving so much and alone."

"It's crossed my mind. I love it here. I love Willow Acres."

"Whatever you decide, know that you have a room at my place if you don't want to live with mom and Aunt D."

"Speaking of Aunt D, have you seen her lately?"

"Yes, she's gone on several dates with Paul since she met him. He seems like a good guy to her. I like him."

"Yeah, they make a great couple. It's time Aunt D started dating again. She had been so hung up on that principal from Atlanta for so long."

"See, love happens when you least expect it," Melanie said with a slight giggle.

"I know. So, want to pass by the Busy Bee for a cappuccino?" Tiffany asked.

"Tiff, are you kidding me? We're still working out!" Melanie said as she rolled her eyes but smiled and said, "Oh, alright. You know we love coffee."

Melanie needed little pressure to stop the workout early. They quickly got off their Stairmasters and headed to the Busy Bee. Melanie and Tiffany enjoyed their cappuccinos at an outdoor table.

"I love the mountain air," Melanie said as she took a deep breath and stretched her legs. She hoped she wouldn't be sore.

"Hello, ladies," Mrs. Adelman said as she got out of her car.

"Hi, Mrs. Adelman," they said at the same time.

Tiffany quickly jumped up and went to help her.

"How is little Ryder?" Mrs. Adelman said as she made her way over to their table.

"He's great. Mom is taking care of him today."

"It's nice to see you both. Please say hi to Mary Elle for

me," Mrs. Adelman said as she answered her cell phone and hurried to speak on the phone.

"That was strange," Tiffany said.

It wasn't like Mrs. Adelman to take a call while she was with others. That was entirely out of character for her.

"Yeah, it must be something important," Melanie said as she finished her cappuccino, "it's late, and I miss my boy. Let's go."

* * *

MELANIE WENT to Mary Elle's after her outing with Tiffany to pick up Ryder. She was singing him to sleep in her arms as she looked out the window when suddenly there was a truck outside the house delivering what seemed like a complete garden with flowers of many kinds.

"Mom, did you order some flowers?" Melanie asked, thinking that maybe they had gotten the wrong address.

"Oh yes, I did. It's for tomorrow's dinner," Mary Elle said nonchalantly.

"New Year's dinner?" Melanie asked, raising her brow.

"Yes, dear, tomorrow's a big day. It's New Year's," Mary Elle said with a shrug as if she was unsure why Melanie was making such a big deal.

"I think you went overboard. They are unloading a ton of flowers," Melanie said as she peered out the window.

"I want it to be special. This is going to be Sienna's first New Year with us. There can never be enough flowers. I'm also waiting on some other things for tomorrow."

"What are you planning on doing with them?"

"Don't worry, dear. I also hired someone to help me decorate for tomorrow. She'll be here soon."

"Who did you hire, and how come you hadn't told me it would be a big party?"

"Because it was a surprise. I hired Mrs. Smith from Five Star Event Planning."

"Oh, she's fancy and pricy."

"I know," Mary Elle said with a smile.

"I wonder what you're up to," Melanie said as she squinted her eyes at her.

"It's just a small New Year's dinner that I want to celebrate with all the ones I love. We've all worked hard, and I want to make it extra special. Don't rain on my parade."

"Okay, if you insist," Melanie said, though she still wasn't convinced.

* * *

RITA WAS GETTING ready for Mary Elle's New Year's dinner party when she heard a light knock at the door. She quickly put her bathrobe on and ran down the stairs. She was hopeful that it would be Alexander.

When she opened the door, she found Sienna standing there.

"Sienna, I'm so glad you could make it. You look amazing," Rita said, giving Sienna a small twirl to get a better look at her dress.

"Thank you," Sienna said, giving Rita a quick hug.

"Bob and I are still getting ready," Rita said as she stood in her bathrobe, letting Sienna in.

"It's ok; I'll hang out with Penny," Sienna said as she leaned down to pet Penny on the head.

Penny didn't waste time and laid on her back to get belly rubs.

"You silly girl. Do you want pets? Who wants pets?" Sienna told Penny, sounding identical to how Rita's baby talked to Penny.

"Sienna, sweet daughter. I thought it was Rita babying

Penny again," Bob said as he entered the living room and placed a kiss on Sienna's cheek.

"Bob, it's nice to see you. You look dashing," Sienna said as she took him in.

"You are too kind," Bob replied with a wink.

"Are the others coming tonight as well?"

"Andrew and Amanda should be here soon. I am not sure if Alexander will be joining us. He still isn't taking our calls," Bob said with a sad sigh.

"I'm so sorry about what happened with Alexander."

"It's okay. He's a good kid. He'll come around."

"I hope you're right, Bob. I still feel strange because of how things happened last time."

"Don't worry. I'm sure it'll be easier this time," Bob said, reassuring Sienna.

Shortly after, Andrew and Amanda walked in.

"I love your dress!" Amanda said as soon as she walked in and spotted Sienna.

"Thank you. I got it at a thrift store for ten dollars," Sienna said shyly.

"Really? I didn't know they sold things like that at a thrift store. You should take me with you next time."

"Ok, I'm ready. Let's get going before we are late," Rita said as she grabbed her purse and shawl.

When she walked into the living room, she caught sight of Amanda and Andrew.

"You made it!" Rita said as she rushed over to them and planted a kiss on each of them.

"Rita, my darling, you look beautiful," Bob said as he kissed her hand, and Rita blushed.

"Oh, Bob, stop it; You'll make me cry, and my makeup will be ruined," Rita said, already dabbing at the corner of her eyes.

"Those two are so adorable," Sienna said to Amanda as they left the house and got into the car.

* * *

MARY ELLE HAD BEEN RUNNING AROUND FRANTICALLY all morning. She had all the décor and floral arrangements set up. She planned a special surprise for everyone and wanted it to go off without a hitch.

"Mary Elle, calm down," Thomas said as he came around and wrapped his arms around her waist.

"I am calm. If I sit still, I'll drive myself crazy. How does it look?" Mary Elle said as she glanced at her backyard, where Mrs. Smith was still working her magic.

Mary Elle tried her hardest to stay out of the way, but it was hard. She was a total control freak when it came to her events.

The New Year's party was being held in her backyard. The teams Mrs. Smith brought had set up the tables and chairs. They made the floral arrangements and waited for the caterers to come with the food.

"It looks beautiful," Thomas said as he kissed her forehead, "and you look breathtaking."

Mary Elle looked down at her pink dress and blushed. Thomas always knew how to make her feel special.

"You're so handsome. I can't believe you're all mine," Mary Elle said as she fixed his suit's collar.

"Hello," a soft voice said from behind him.

Thomas and Mary Elle jumped apart like two teenagers that had just been caught sneaking around.

"Wyatt!" Mary Elle and Thomas both exclaimed.

"I can't believe you made it," Thomas said as he pulled the young boy into a hug and ruffled his hair.

"I'm so happy to see you. We've missed you so much," Mary Elle said as she took her turn hugging him.

"I'm sorry that I left the way I did," Wyatt said as he looked down at his feet.

"You don't need to apologize. We understand you were dealing with a lot. We're just happy to have you back," Thomas said, slinging an arm around his shoulders.

Wyatt was only 16 years old and worked as a server at the restaurant in Willow Acres. After missing workdays without calling in and even stealing from them, he moved to Tennessee to live with his grandmother. Thomas and Mary Elle had been extremely worried about him because his behavior was so out of character.

When a CPC worker showed up at Willow Acres, they discovered that his mother had abandoned him and left him with no electricity or running water. As soon as the CPC worker left, Thomas called Wyatt and apologized for not stepping in or helping him sooner. Since his grandmother was in a nursing home and Wyatt lived alone, she asked Thomas to step in as his legal guardian. Wyatt would now live with Thomas and would go back to school.

* * *

"WE'RE HERE!" Melanie and Tiffany called out as they stepped into their mother's home.

"Girls, I'm in the kitchen!" Mary Elle called out.

"Mom! You look so beautiful," Melanie said as she touched her mother's hair.

"Thomas is one lucky man," Tiffany said as she looked over at her mother with her pretty shimmery pink dress.

"How do I look?" DeeAnn asked as she stroked a pose at the end of the staircase.

All the ladies oohed and ahhed over each other's outfits for a few more minutes before Mary Elle put them to work.

Mary Elle and Thomas mingled with the guests for a little while before disappearing. They had gone to the backyard to take some photos and then returned to take several pictures with family and friends by the Christmas tree. Mary Elle then once again quietly disappeared.

"Mom?" Tiffany said, standing outside Mary Elle's bedroom door.

"Yes, Tiffany," Mary Elle called out.

"The guests are arriving. Are you ready to come downstairs?"

"She'll be ready in a second," Mrs. Smith said as she poked her head out the door without letting Tiffany inside or take a peek.

"Ok, what do I tell them?"

"Tiffany, there's a small reception area in the living room where the guests can mingle until Mary Elle is ready," Mrs. Smith said as she tried to get rid of Tiffany.

"Ok, and they look up their table on the chart?"

"Yes, Tiffany. We have three tables for the guests. I'll be right out to help you," Mrs. Smith said.

Tiffany went downstairs and found Melanie, Rita, Bob, Cade, Sienna, and David.

"Mrs. Smith said mom's still getting ready," Tiffany informed everyone.

"Where's Thomas?" Melanie asked, looking around.

"Not sure. I haven't seen him. We can have some appetizers while we wait for mom and Thomas and the other guests," Tiffany suggested.

"Mary Elle, are you alright?" Rita called at Mary Elle's bedroom door.

"Yes, Rita. I'm ok. I'll be out in a minute, just finishing my makeup," Mary Elle said.

"Well, okay. We'll be downstairs waiting for you," Rita said and was a little hurt that Mary Elle wasn't letting her in the room.

As Rita got to the bottom of the stairs, she ran into Alexander.

"Alexander," Rita said and felt tears forming in her eyes.

She'd never been so happy to see him. She wanted to throw her arms around him but held herself back.

"Hi, Mom," he said.

"Alex, it's nice to see you again," Bob said as he walked over to them.

"Mary Elle said she would never forgive me if I didn't come today, and she can be a kind of scary when she wants to be," Alexander said with a sheepish smile.

No one said anything for a few seconds, but it felt like an eternity.

"I would like to speak to you privately," Alexander said.

"We can step outside if you'd like," Rita said as she grabbed her coat from the coat rack and stepped outside.

"Mom, Dad, I came by to apologize. I feel horrible about my reaction. I was out of line and rude." Alexander said as he pushed the snow around with his shoe. "I was just in shock about Sienna and everything. I've been emotional recently, and I guess I felt that maybe your love for us would have changed once Sienna came into your life. But I now realize that's a childish thought and that your love for us is uncondi-tional. I'm embarrassed about my behavior and am truly sorry for hurting your feelings and accusing Sienna of being something she isn't. I'll apologize to her when I see her."

"It's ok, Alexander. We forgive you," Rita said as she hugged him.

She knew holidays were always rough on him. He always wondered what had happened to Emma. They all did, but he took it the hardest.

"Come here," Bob said as he gestured for Alex to come in for a hug, "We will always love you, and you will always be our son, no matter what."

"Thank you," Alexander said with tears in his eyes.

* * *

Everyone sat around Mary Elle's living room, wondering what was taking so long. They all quieted as they saw Mrs. Smith come down the stairs and focus on her.

"Welcome all to Mary Elle and Thomas' New Year dinner and wedding," Mrs. Smith said to everyone's surprise.

"Wedding?" everyone was asking.

"Yes, their wedding. They wanted to surprise their close friends and family with this gift. Please enjoy the reception and kindly look for your names for the seating arrangements and we will begin the ceremony shortly," Mrs. Smith said as the catering company appeared out of thin air.

"I can't believe mom didn't tell us!" Melanie said with a mixture of surprise and shock.

"We didn't see this coming, that's for sure," Tiffany said as she noticed Michael and Thomas walking in together.

"Michael, you're here," his sisters said as they both rushed to greet him.

"I'm here. Where's mom?"

"She's getting ready. It's her wedding tonight," Tiffany told Michael in case he hadn't heard the gasps and everyone repeatedly muttering the word "wedding," all confused.

"I know. Thomas just told me outside. He wanted me to be the best man, but I said no, it should be David."

"What did Thomas say about that?" Melanie asked.

"Thomas said he would ask David since I said no."

"I guess that's what he's talking to David about now. I

hope you weren't rude in declining his offer to be his best man." Melanie said, knowing that Michael was too abrasive.

"I explained that I didn't feel like I could be his best man because I didn't know him that well. I told him that both David and Cade knew him and his mom. They had been sharing special moments with them instead of me. He understood and was satisfied with my reasoning," Michael said, sounding sincere.

"Well, you have a point. I hope you did the right thing for mom's sake," Tiffany said, hoping nothing would ruin their mom's wedding.

"Ladies and gentlemen, please find your tables and have a seat. The moment we have been waiting for tonight is about to begin," Mrs. Smith said over a microphone.

The family was there now, including Vera and Willow Acres' close-knit workforce. Mrs. Smith had truly outdone herself on this occasion. She worked her magic by setting everything up inside Mary Elle's house and backyard. Everything was elegant and perfectly matched Mary Elle's personality and taste.

Thomas was standing at the end of the aisle towards Mary Elle's in the backyard, where Mrs. Smith had placed a beautiful wooden arch with all-natural flowers and draping sheer white linen. The table centerpieces were natural white roses with light pink roses, peonies, the star of Bethlehem, Queen Anne's lace, and greenery with a small candle inside a glass in the middle. Décor was simple yet elegant, just like Mary Elle. Thomas looked nervous but happy. David joined him, and they exchanged smiles. The photographer suddenly appeared and started taking photos, and his assistant helped take some video footage of the guests, food, and small details, among other things.

CHAPTER 12

*E*veryone stood as *At Last* by Etta James came on. No other song could describe how Mary Elle felt about finally finding love, her true love. This love she felt and had for Thomas was unlike anything she had ever felt. It was not teen hormones that drove this feeling; it was a conscious decision to open her heart and let love flow.

Mary Elle walked down the aisle in a beautiful off-white Bardot neckline dress with ¾ sleeve, a delicate embroidered fitted bodice, and a godet-detail skirt. Her hair was in a soft, gorgeous bun with tiny off-white pearls sparsely adorning her hair. The small bouquet she held was full of Mary Elle's favorite white and pink roses, peonies, gardenias, Queen Anne's lace, and eucalyptus with other greenery added.

As Mary Elle walked down the aisle on Michael's arm, she looked at all her guests and smiled. Nothing meant more to her than seeing all her loved ones gather to witness her wedding day. When she glanced at the end of the aisle, she found Thomas wiping happy tears off his cheeks. *Her Thomas,* the one that had showed her what true love meant. The one that pieced her heart back together and held it in his hands. He was standing underneath the wooden arch Mrs. Smith had set up. DeeAnn, the maid of honor, stood to one side and David next to Thomas. The sun was setting, and the ambiance was perfect. There was no snow; it was a lovely day with mild temperature. She thanked God for hearing her prayer about having nice weather today. When she reached the end of the aisle, Thomas took her hands in his.

"Dearly beloved, we are gathered here in the sight of God and in the face of this company of witnesses to join together this man and this woman in Holy Matrimony..." Pastor Miller began.

Mary Elle and Thomas stared into each other's eyes, and every little memory played back in her mind. The first time she saw Thomas at the restaurant in Willow Acres, and he offered her a job, the time he took her to the overlook, and the time she realized she was madly and deeply in love with him when she saw him around the fire with her kids telling stories and sharing laughs. Why had it taken a car accident to realize that she was being a fool?

Pastor Miller broke into Mary Elle's thought when he said, "The bride and groom have written their vows and will recite them now, Thomas," he said, signaling Thomas to go ahead.

"In all my days, I've never met a woman who has captivated me the way you have, Mary Elle. I could not be more honored to pledge myself to you. I promise to protect you, to provide for you. I promise to show you how much you mean to me daily. I promise I will never love another or look at another. I will be your husband until the Lord takes me from this world. The day I die, everyone will be able to testify to how much I loved you. You are my world, Mary Elle," Thomas said as his voice cracked many times.

"Thomas, words cannot describe how much I love you and how grateful I am that God brought you into my life. I came confident you are the man the Lord has chosen just for me. You have pledged your love and life to me on this day, and I gladly pledge always to love you and honor you. You are my best friend, and I cannot wait to live the rest of my life with you. You will forever be my greatest gift," Mary Elle said, and Thomas gave her hand a small squeeze while he mouthed the words, *I love you.*

Pastor Miller had them exchange rings before saying, "You may now kiss the bride!"

Thomas placed his hands on both sides of her face and kissed her tenderly. When they parted, they turned to face their loved ones, and Thomas raised her hand in the air and yelled, "Mrs. Clarke, ladies, and gentlemen!" as everyone ran over to hug and kiss them.

* * *

As everyone was distracted congratulating Mary Elle and Thomas, Alexander went in search of Sienna. He found her by the champagne fountain.

"Sienna?" he mumbled.

Sienna turned to him, and an uneasy look crossed her face when she realized who it was.

"I wanted to apologize to you," Alexander said.

"Okay."

"I'm sorry about the things I said. I didn't think you would hear me, which doesn't make it right."

"It's okay," Sienna said, placing a hand on his arm to stop him from apologizing.

"No, it's not. I had a tough upbringing, and I've always had difficulty expressing myself. Sometimes I lash out without thinking. That night at the house, I knew it was wrong, and I shouldn't be acting that way, but I couldn't control myself."

Sienna nodded but said nothing.

Alexander sighed. "My siblings and I were abandoned at a young age, which scars you for the rest of your life. As a kid, I always feared the day that Rita and Bob would abandon us, too. When they told us you were their daughter and were back in their life, all those feelings came rushing back to me, and I'm so sorry I took it out on you."

"Alexander, I am so sorry that you went through that. I hold nothing against you. I want to have a relationship with you and the rest of the family. Do you think we can start over?"

"If you can forgive me, yes," he said.

"In my mind, that night never happened. It is erased from my memory," Sienna said with a smile.

"Thank you," Alexander said with a crack in his voice.

"A hug?" Sienna asked.

Alexander hugged her and said, "Welcome to the family, sis."

* * *

"Hi there, Mrs. Clarke," Tiffany said as she hugged her mother and tried not to cry.

"Mrs. Clarke, oh boy!" Mary Elle said with a giddy laugh.

"Mom, you look stunning," Melanie said as she hugged her.

"Mary Elle, had you been planning this wedding all along and acted like you were dragging your feet to throw us off?" Rita asked, pulling Mary Elle to the side.

"No, not at all. I was dragging my feet. Everything changed the moment we were told about the car accident at Christmas. I realized any of us could be gone in an instant and that I was being completely unreasonable."

"I'm glad you came to your senses," Rita said as she pulled her best friend into another hug.

Rita and Mary Elle stood and watched everyone they loved mingling. All their kids were taking selfies and sharing jokes, even Sienna. Bob and Thomas shared a drink by the bar, and DeeAnn was on the dance floor with Paul. A server passed by with a tray of drinks, and the ladies each got one.

"I would like to make a small toast," Rita said.

"Okay."

"To our kids," Rita said as she glanced over at them. She couldn't believe that her dream of having them all together had finally come true. She had prayed for this moment all their life. "Who give us gray hairs, but we love all the same. They teach us how to love unconditionally."

"To our men," Mary Elle said as she looked over at Thomas and Bob, who were hugging. She continued, "Who are lucky to have us, and we are lucky to be loved by."

"To sisters," DeeAnn said as she appeared with a glass of her own, "Who teach us forgiveness and acceptance for who we are and that family isn't only blood but those we choose to go through life with."

Mary Elle wrapped an arm around each of their waists. Her girls. She wouldn't change this last year for anything at all. God's faithfulness was evident yet again in their lives. For the upcoming year, she would take all the love and the happy memories that had brought them here today. Next year would be full of more surprises and more hardships, but she knew there was nothing they couldn't get through if they placed God at the center and relied on each other for support.

EPILOGUE

$\mathcal{M}$ary Elle brought a pot roast from the oven and placed it on the kitchen island. She was now living with Thomas and Wyatt, and life couldn't get any better than this. It was family Sunday at Willow Acres, so the entire gang was coming together again. Family Sundays were her absolute favorite. There was no talk of work allowed. They ate, played games, and enjoyed each other's company. This was the first time she and Thomas would see the gang since they returned from their month-long honeymoon in Ireland.

She couldn't wait to see everyone, especially little Ryder. He was only three months old but was already teething. Cade had arrived earlier to help Mary Elle set up a slideshow to show her honeymoon photos. The rest of the gang would be here, too, with their families. Thomas and Mary Elle kept in touch with everyone while they were away. Bob and Rita's relationship with Sienna improved daily, and their kids got along great.

The snow was falling outside, and everything was covered in white. The snowflakes were falling heavy and fast, but the fire was burning, and the dining table was set up. The first to show up was Tiffany and David. David had gone to pick her up at the airport.

"Hi, mom!" Tiffany said as she walked in the door, her hair covered in snow. She even had snow on her eyelashes.

"My littlest baby! How I've missed you!" Mary Elle said as she pulled her into a deep embrace.

"I've missed you! Video calls are not the same as face-to-face," Tiffany said as she made herself comfortable on the sofa.

"Thank you for picking her up, David."

David was too busy stuffing an apple in his mouth to respond, but he squeezed her shoulder. That boy was always eating. He quickly headed back out on his way to bring Mrs. Adelman and Mrs. Waskosky to the get-together.

Patty walked in next with Lisa, Dean, and Jasper.

"Mary Elle, you're glowing," Lisa said as they hugged.

"The gangs all here!" Thomas said as he came in and hugged everyone.

Melanie, Cade, and Ryder came in next, followed by Bob and Rita. DeeAnn and her official boyfriend Paul also came by with chips, dip, and the game of risk.

Once everyone was gathered, Mary Elle said, "Thomas and I want to welcome you all into our home. We wanted to announce that we are Wyatt's legal guardians now, and he will go back to school soon. We also wanted to share a quick slideshow with all the photos of our trip to Ireland."

"Mom, we are so glad you and Thomas are back. We missed you so much!" Melanie said with a twinkle in her eye.

"Hi there, little bro," Tiffany called out to Wyatt as he stood across the room, shyly waving back.

They all took their seats on The Big U-shaped sofa Thomas and Mary Elle specifically picked out for moments like this when everyone was gathered around. Mary Elle took her seat next to Thomas, and he wrapped an arm around her.

She rested her head on his chest, and he hit play on the remote. The large tv began to display large photos of their trip. From the moment they got to the airport to all the moments in between. She looked up and caught Thomas staring down at her. He leaned down and kissed her forehead. Every little moment in her life had brought her to this point. All the good and the bad had led her to this man who loved her with all his heart. Life couldn't be sweeter for Mary Elle and her loved ones. This moment, surrounded by all they held near and dear, was exactly what life was about.

THANK you for reading Christmas in Willow Heights. I hope you enjoyed it! Your support means the world to me. The next book in the series is The Inn at Willow Heights. Click here if you'd like to join Mary Elle and the rest of the gang in the next book. The fifth book in the series, The Wedding at Willow Heights, can be found here.

Let's be friends!

Join Abigail's Newsletter for reminders of upcoming releases.

JOIN ABIGAIL'S Reader Group for: First Looks, exclusive giveaways, and more!